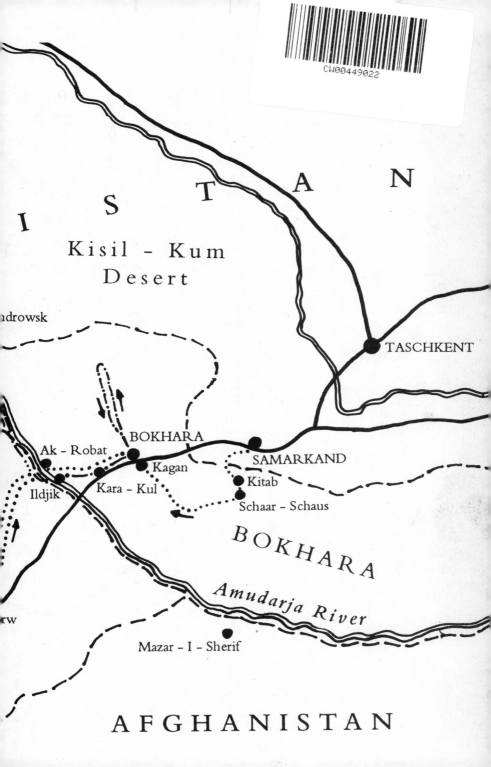

*My Golden Road
from Samarkand*

My Golden Road from Samarkand

Jascha Golowanjuk

Translated by Henning Koch

QUARTET BOOKS

First published in Great Britain by Quartet Books Limited 1993
A member of the Namara Group
27/29 Goodge Street
London W1P 1FD

Originally published in Sweden under the title *Min Gyllene Vag
Fran Samarkand*
Copyright © by Jascha Golowanjuk Estate 1978
Translation copyright © by Henning Koch 1993

A catalogue record for this title is available from the British
Library

ISBN 0 7043 7039 5

Typeset by The Electronic Book Factory Ltd, Fife, Scotland
Printed and bound in Great Britain by
BPCC Hazell Books Ltd
Member of BPCC Ltd

Contents

I

My Childhood is Terminated by the Revolution

There can only be a handful of people in this world able to harken back to an exact moment in their lives when childhood ended, and, simultaneously, adulthood began. I am able to do so. For me, the prescribed hour was three o'clock, on the last day of May 1917, in Saratoff. I was on my way to the Conservatory, where I was studying, with a violin tucked under one arm and a bundle of music under the other. The day's task was a recital of Mendelssohn's violin concerto. My teacher, who was rather severe, had required me to learn the piece by heart, and I, as many an eleven-year-old would have, felt a certain amount of trepidation. The last few bars were repeatedly playing through my mind, and I suppose that I was proceeding in the manner of a sleepwalker.

Then, all at once, I was brought to my senses by the crack of a gun. I heard the plaintive whistling of a bullet passing close to my ear. This shot, and this moment, brought my childhood to an end.

Instinctively, I shielded my head. As the first shot was immediately followed by a barrage of others, I followed the example of every other pedestrian in the street: without looking back, I fell in with the desperate mob and ran for cover.

To begin with, I did not understand the significance of this event. I knew that my motherland Russia was engaged in a blistering war with Germany, but surely it could not be the Germans who were already marching into Saratoff?

It was impossible to move freely amid the streams of people gripped by panic. Where could one go to escape the hungry bullets whistling about one's ears? The frenzied crowd rushed into a side-street; although people to my left and right were taking cover in doorways, cellars, and any other available crannies, I was carried forward on a wave of human bodies towards the Conservatory. The sight of the familiar building was enough to fill me with hope. A few moments ago I had thought of my lesson with a great deal of anxiety, but now the Conservatory symbolised an escape from death.

At the front portal, I discovered an older classmate beckoning me. He was a pleasant but talentless boy, dubbed by our professor 'the man with tin-plate eyes', because whenever his style of playing was denigrated (something which happened almost every day) his eyes would widen in dismay. But I had never before seen his colourless eyes so large and round and full of terror. A woman running before me suddenly dropped like a sack at my feet. I jumped over her and into the arms of my friend, who squeezed me so that I could barely breathe. To this day I do not know whether he was shielding my body or his own!

There was a large notice on the door of the Conservatory. 'Closed' I read. When I asked my friend what this could mean, he did not answer. His eyes were like cups filled with terror; he was staring at a nearby garden. From there the smoke of the shots was rising, and then I saw the marksmen – a group of soldiers whose volleys had by now largely swept the streets clean. Bullets were still buzzing all about us. Suddenly my friend's arms relinquished their hold on my waist. I looked up at his face. His mouth was open but not a sound came from his lips. His eyes were as expressionless as ever. Between them I noticed a small round hole, no bigger than a kopeck coin. Slowly, he slid to the ground, and when his head tilted forward on to his chest, I realised that the back of his cranium had been blasted off – the work of a dum-dum bullet. In horror, I let go of my bundle of music. Death had literally held me in its arms, but it had let go. Another volley of bullets whizzed past me, reminding me that my turn was next. Somehow I found the strength and will to drag my paralysed legs across the exposed street towards an open gateway that I discerned as if through a dense fog. I toppled through the doorway where a good thirty people cowered, as pale and fearful as I. An old woman with wiry arms dragged me into the yard; holding me in her arms, she sank down on to a barrel.

'By Our Heavenly Father, this is the Revolution!' And she shook me, and asked me severely: '*Maltjik* [little boy], what are you doing on the streets when the devil is abroad? You should be at home saying your prayers!'

I told her how close I had come to death, and about the loss of my friend with the tin-plate eyes. The day before yesterday he had given me a picture of Isaiah and today he lay at the front of the Conservatory with the back of his head blown off! Was it not bad enough to have to play scales and do homework for the professors? Did I have to be shot as well? Would I ever see my mama and papa again? Did Babushka think that it was the Germans who were taking Saratoff? I could speak some German too . . . *Bitte sehr* . . . *liebes Fräulein* . . . *Guten Tag* . . . *Auf Wiedersehen* . . . *Lausbube*! Did Babushka think the shooting would continue all day?

'Hold your stupid mouth! A big boy like you shouldn't sit there and talk such rubbish! You tell me where you live, little one, and I'll walk home with you as soon as this unholy shooting stops . . . !' From the depths of her petticoats she fished out a jam *piroshki* wrapped in newspaper. This, in maternal fashion, she shared with me. It was all we had that day, for the shooting continued until darkness fell, and only then did we dare leave the safety of our yard and go back into the street. The *babushka* held me firmly by the hand. I was still clutching my violin.

It was a grisly, meandering journey over dead people and through pools of sticky blood. There was no moon, no light cast over the slaughter. The night was full of sobbing, moaning, and anguished cries.

My elderly guardian angel delivered me into the hands of the fat Jewess with whom I was boarding. She gave me her blessing as she said her farewell and, in truth, I must have needed it: as soon as the door had closed, the Jewess welcomed me by thoroughly cuffing me and boxing my ears. After all the happenings of that day, I remember, this punishment did not pain me in the least. It was a mere expression of the anguish she had felt for the safety of her protégé.

The extent of her terror was proved by the fact that her hair turned grey over the next twenty-four hours. The poor woman believed that the disturbances in Saratoff augured another Jewish pogrom; she had already experienced such a thing after the 1905 Japanese War, and although she had escaped with her life, the horrors of it had never left her.

On the following day she managed to send a telegram to my parents, in which she explained that she could no longer vouch for my life. She demanded that I return home immediately.

Thus my childhood was over. Death had let me slip out of its embrace, only to throw me into even more dangerous, and even more frightful adventures.

2

The Final Journey to Samarkand

I had been at the Conservatory in Saratoff for four years, and each term had made the six-day journey from Samarkand and back. The passage was therefore well known to me, but on this occasion it seemed entirely new, thanks to the turbulent events in Russia. It began with the cab driver demanding double the normal fare to drive me to the quay for the first stage of the journey: a boat-trip down the Volga to Samara. The porter who took my trunk on board was similarly dissatisfied – when I handed him the usual twenty kopecks, he waved his fist in front of me and shouted: 'Little brother, are you going mad, this won't buy so much as a box of matches . . .' And, as if to soften his own severity, he quite amicably stuck out his tongue.

That was the last I saw of Saratoff!

In Samara I was to continue by train, and here my real difficulties began. Not even with offers of doubled fares could I entice a hackney driver to take me and my heavy luggage to the station. My limited funds prevented me from making any higher offers. There I stood, small and helpless with my trunk and violin by the banks of the Volga, while people ran to and fro, frenziedly shouting. As so many times before, a benefactor came along when my prospects were at their gloomiest. On this occasion he appeared in the form of a long-haired student, moved by my helplessness. With a swift and firm grip, he lifted me and all my accoutrements into a cart and drove me to the steps of the railway station, where in similar fashion he unloaded my things. As a farewell he made a cross on my forehead. Evidently he was an active theologian, putting his studies into practice. Samara Railway Station was as unpleasant as a wasps' nest. Parents were raving and pillaging through the crowd, looking for lost youngsters squealing somewhere beyond obstructing bodies. The cursing, the barking of dogs, yells and furious outbursts from those trodden underfoot, combined in violent cacophony. A widespread terror of the Revolution was sweeping over Russia, and it had reached Samara too. There was a daubed sign on the wall: 'Beware of pickpockets'. My anxious hands wandered between the trunk, the violin case and the wallet, in the vain hope of safeguarding my possessions in this raging sea.

In fifteen minutes the train would leave, and yet there were long queues at every ticket booth. I timidly walked down one such line, keeping an eye on my trunk while watching the faces of the impatient and desperate refugees. Then to my delight, at the very front of the queue, I saw another of those benevolent *babushkas*. She peered at me with twinkling eyes, and within a few seconds I was at her side, quietly pleading with her to buy me a ticket. She nodded soberly, and said: 'Go to your trunk, little *maltjik*, mother's coming in a minute.'

Fretful travellers queuing behind us threw me looks of undiluted hatred, but the sturdy *babushka* reciprocated with a stolid gaze. I was convinced that she must be a fairy godmother in the garb of a peasant. After a few minutes of lingering, she came to me.

'You run to the train and find two seats!' For an instant, I doubted her. Was the fairy perchance an evil witch who intended to steal my trunk? Her little

6

eyes blinked so artlessly at me that I took the risk and elbowed my way through the unyielding crowd, pushing my violin before me as a snow-plough.

The train was packed tight as a tin of anchovies. There was nowhere to sit. However, necessity knows no law, and an empty toilet struck me as highly desirable – no less than a forecourt to paradise itself! I threw my violin inside, closed the door, and went back in search of my fairy. Evidently she possessed the little folk's talent for disappearing into thin air. I searched for her amongst the human flotsam on the platforms. Where could she be? The first departure bell sounded behind me, and my pulse raced. When the second bell went, five minutes later, my heart was in my mouth. Then I spotted her. She had attached our trunks to a length of rope, and was dragging them along the platform like a carthorse. Her groaning and puffing were in the spirit of a Volga boatman, and I ran to help her, lugging and pushing the load as well as I could. No sooner had we got our effects aboard and stashed them in the lavatory, than the train jerked into motion. She pushed me in as well, for good measure, and closed the door behind me. I tumbled on to the floor, still with the violin in my arms, and fell asleep at once.

In the middle of the night I woke up, and tried in vain to get out of my little cell. There were so many travellers in the corridor that the door would not open. Through a crack in the window I could see that the small ledges between one carriage and the next were crowded with people, many asleep on their feet, kept upright by the crush. On the iron steps passengers were clinging like flies, and on the roof they lay in great droves. Some of these unfortunate people were unable to stay awake, and when the train bounced or jerked suddenly, they slid off with anguished cries into the night.

Towards morning I was able to open the door

sufficiently to slip out into the corridor, where I found my good fairy hunched on the floor, snoring loudly while her unkempt locks kept time with the train's rumblings.

At no time during the journey did a conductor make an appearance. There was no question of asking for tickets, and when we pulled in at Orenburg I discovered that the windows at the back of the train had been shattered. At every station fresh bodies wriggled in through the holed panes, while the doors were crammed with disembarking passengers. In the general pandemonium, the babushka and I took the opportunity of claiming a whole bench for ourselves. Her mortal frame was not a thing to be sniffed at – when she extended her bulk fully, there was no room on the bench for anyone except me! Our place secure, I rushed off in search of food. Our store of sandwiches had long since been depleted, and to make things worse, prices had risen tenfold. However, even those with plenty of money found that there was nothing left to buy; luckily in all Russian railway stations hot water for tea can be procured with a minimum of difficulty, so we silenced our complaining stomachs with glasses of the Russian elixir.

Most of the passengers felt unable even to fetch tea-water, in view of the rivalry for seats. But I, with the loyal fairy babushka guarding my seat, rushed in and out of the train with hot water, helping as many people as I could. For my services as a water-bearer I was rewarded with bread and sugar, a welcome addition to our meagre supplies.

At a later stop a wealthy Kirghiz entered our compartment with his two wives in tow. He wore heavy silver rings on his fingers and a thick gold chain about his waist. His wives both had silver rings in their noses, and one, apparently his favourite, had threaded a silver coin on to hers, which dangled in front of her beautiful lips.

When she was eating, she stuffed it unceremoniously into one nostril, so that she could enjoy unhindered the rinds of cheese and bits of bread-crust that her spouse condescended to throw to her. Truthfully it looked no more civilized than when one throws bread to monkeys in a cage. These women sat crouched on the floor like little wild animals, and if by chance they got in the way of anyone, they were kicked and cursed without the least reaction from their husband and protector. He was far too absorbed in his white goat's cheese!

The further south we went, the more stifling and hot it became. By this time, the windows in our carriage had also been knocked out, but for this we were frankly grateful: before, the air had been too potent to breathe on account of the odours and exhalations given off by our unfortunate band of travellers. Perhaps it was only my imagination, but it seemed to me that the train was steaming onwards at an ever-slowing pace, as if it also felt the strain of these endless nights and days. Although we were still in the month of May, the steppe had been burned to cinders by the sun. In places I could see flaming red patches of poppy – for even the steppe wished to clothe itself in the colour of the Revolution.

The lack of provisions was becoming a major concern. Most of us had set off in a frenzied hurry, and there had been no time to worry about provender. And, what with the absence of supplies at the stations, and with the timespan of the journey stretched out over days, no amount of sharing could still our raging appetites.

Early one morning the train rolled into the station by the Aral Sea, and all along the platform a gang of fishermen's wives had piled great mounds of fried fish. Was this an hallucination? Roaring with joy, a trainful of passengers threw themselves out of the doors, and within a few minutes all the fish, as if by magic, had gone. Imagine the rejoicing when a few Kirghiz

9

men appeared soon after, bearing a great supply of *kumis* (fermented horse's milk which in many parts of Russia is considered a true delicacy!). It did not take long for the Kirghiz to sell all their stock and it was an almost satiated train that chugged on towards the East. I, however, was not one of these contented people, for my finances did not permit me any culinary extravagances.

An Armenian family had boarded the train and entered our compartment. They arranged themselves around a large wickerwork hamper, whose lid the father lifted with reverence. Once again I thought I was seeing things; he eased out a huge grilled goose, and with his fingers began to peel off strips of succulent meat for his family. I was bewitched, and could not avert my eyes from this heavenly vision that made the saliva rise in my mouth. The silent plea of my hungry eyes must have touched his heart, because all of a sudden he took a firm hold of a drumstick, ripped it off, and handed it to me with a kindly nod. I almost swooned with joy! This princely gift I consumed with voluptuous abandon and soon my hands and face were smeared in rich goose fat which, to my sorrow, I was ordered to clean off. But where to find water? I knew there had not been a drop of water in the toilet for three days. On the other hand it was possible that the tanks had been replenished at the station, blessed by its proximity to the Aral Sea.

I went to the toilet and opened the door, but before I could as much as blink an arm had hauled me inside. In front of me stood a uniformed officer. He smiled to put me at my ease, and then said, 'Little boy, do you have any buttons?'

I answered that the only ones I had were on my shirt and trousers. In a moment he had unsheathed a knife, snipped off my buttons and, with a dexterous hand, substituted his own gilded studs for mine. So intent was he on this task, and so serious, that it did not occur to me to question him about his behaviour. When he was done he gave me a silver rouble (a rare sight at this time) and kissed my forehead with the words, 'Do not betray me, little friend . . .' Thereafter he pushed me out again and closed the door. I stood covered in goose fat as before, but a good deal more handsome in my gold buttons.

When later in the day I saw this mysterious officer again, he was transformed. In his regimental shirt I recognised my trouser buttons, his epaulettes had been torn off, the peaked cap was gone, and his hair hung dishevelled across his face. Even the erect military posture had been carefully discarded. He threw an imploring glance at me, and laid a finger across his lips. Although I was only a child, I was filled with pride to be part of this man's secret. Maybe I had helped save his life?

The train continued through the endless steppes of Turkestan. The parched earth stretched further than the eye could see, without the solace of a single tree or shadow. From a cloudless sky the sun poured forth, and the carriages were hot as bread-ovens. Hour after hour I watched the sweeping parade of telegraph poles; at times we passed through sandy desert, with miles and miles of reed matting erected on both sides of the railway tracks to prevent them from being buried by the constantly moving sand. A whirling storm of sand and dust was sucked in through the shattered windows, so that we were covered in an inch-thick layer of granular debris which stung our eyes. And from the sandy banks and cuttings along our route, hundreds of thousands of tortoises had issued from their holes and crawled on to the tracks to partake of the sun, only to be crushed wholesale under our frenzied wheels which finally became red and shiny with splattered blood. The burning sun, the oven-like heat, the blistering

11

flying sand and the bright blood shimmered in front of my eyes like a fire. Was this a journey without end? Although we had travelled without pause for almost a week, we were still days behind schedule. Yet, delay was something that all Russians readily accepted, indeed, even counted on.

At last we arrived as Taschkent, the largest oasis in Turkestan. There were few signs of the revolution here: no uniforms, at least. But the Russian twin eagle over the main entrance had been smeared with red paint. I had to change trains at Taschkent. It was time to say farewell to my 'fairy godmother'.

The old woman had been the most loyal and kind companion. She had shared everything with me, up to her last slice of bread. Over the last few days we had tried to quicken time by recounting every story and fairytale that we knew, but at the end we had fallen prey to a dull torpor. Heat, thirst and hunger had metamorphosed us into a pair of senseless dry clods of clay, who at the moment of their parting suddenly came to life again, just in time to exchange a few words.

'Say your prayers every night, *maltjik*, and go to church like a good Christian, and then the Revolution will not be able to touch you,' she advised tearfully. When the train pulled away, she was weeping; I watched her hanging out of the window, waving with her dirty grey head-shawl. To others she may have been a comical figure, but to me she was without question a creature of legend. I have never seen her again. However, I would soon learn that her theories about the Revolution were, at the very least, divorced from reality.

After several hours of waiting for my train, and another night of travelling, I finally arrived back home. The journey had taken nine days instead of the usual six. Starving, utterly dehydrated, and without a kopeck in

12

my pocket, I descended from the train at Samarkand. I saw someone coming towards me, and then I was enveloped in strong welcoming arms. All my struggles and fears were forgotten at once in the arms of my father.

3

The Dream City

I know that for a European there is magic in the mere utterance of the name: Samarkand! The passing years have borne me far from its hinterland, and yet the name of Samarkand sounds in my ears with the resonance of some evocative bell. Samarkand! To me, the city is synonymous with the years of my childhood. The clear, tender light in which those times seem steeped, harmonises perfectly with the gleam of minarets and domes, standing as in the tales from *A Thousand and One Nights* in their mosaic skirts of red, white, yellow, green and lapis lazuli. The bazaars, the *madrasahs*, and the mosques uphold the myth of Samarkand as a focal point of the Eastern world's mystique. The most beautiful mosques are found amongst a congeries of venerable buildings around the Registan, a central square. These are generally of sixteenth- and seventeenth-century origin. Older buildings are either decrepit or in ruins. Among the fourteenth- and fifteenth-century ruins, the mausoleum of Timor and his family must be singled out, as must his monument to a favourite wife, the Chinese princess Bibi Khanum. Its ruins are marked by a melancholic and enchanted beauty. Half of one dome still stands undamaged, painted in a fresco of sky-blue, and in spring its hue merges with the warm sky in remarkable harmony.

On the outskirts of the old city lies the surprisingly

humble domed tomb of Gur-Emir, where Timor rests after his fierce life. The largest block of nephrite in the world covers his grave.

Not far from here is the so-called Zinda, an oubliette dungeon. It resembles a well with narrow rim, but expands downwards into a large pit with sheer walls. In previous times, criminals were flung into this pit and left to die. Merciful passers-by may have thrown down bread and fruit to the unfortunate prisoners, and once per day a pot of water was lowered – but this would only have prolonged the agony of those below. Russian administration has since forbidden this cruel practice. After darkness had fallen, one always hurried past the old Zinda. It was rumoured that if, during the full moon, one put an ear to the ground, complaints and groans of pain could still be heard.

The imposing Arabic buildings from an eclipsed age of greatness make the rest of Samarkand seem unremarkable. Large it may be, and extensive its streets, but nevertheless all of the houses are constructed of clay. A prolonged downpour could wash away the larger part of the Old Town. Whenever it does rain, massive clay basins are always placed in the middle of the huts to collect the water that seeps through the roofs.

The bazaar, in all its glory, consists of a jumble of houses and magazines around thoroughfares and alleys covered over with mats of branchwork and plaited grass to guard the offered wares from an ever-watchful enemy – the sun. In the gloomy passages underneath, the great caravans press on; each camel bears its own bell, making a loud and tuneless ringing. The animals are loaded with astrakhan furs from Turkestan, tea from China and spices from India. From time to time a little donkey comes by, bearing such a mountainous load that only its ears are visible. Or a whole family of Sarts may be perched on its patient back, which, remarkably, has not yet snapped. The alarum of the caravans, the howling of dogs, braying of donkeys and goats, neighing of horses, and panicked clucking of poultry, find their equivalent timbre and variety in the human orchestra.

Trade, in the East, is always a noisy affair. Important deals are commonly introduced with a few bowls of strong green tea. It is considered extremely unrefined to buy without bargaining, and this occurs with such screams and gestures that murder seems imminent. The noise begins at five in the morning, or even earlier in the summer, and continues until sundown. Here the Kirghiz market their livestock, the Chinese their porcelain, the Indians their spices, here the proud Afghanis with stately bearing and in high turbans saunter about and carry out their currency trading. The Turks make their entrance in enormous black fleece caps protecting them from the desert sun, while Persians wear small, neat astrahkan hats. The Sarts, however, make up the dominant strain. They are a lowly, uneducated people, not overly fond of industriousness. Most of them can neither read nor write. The Sart wears a kaftan with arms so long that it obscures the hands which, according to custom, it is uncouth to show. His trousers are well tucked into his boots and around his waist is an intricately embroidered belt or shawl. On his head he wears a turban; beneath this he keeps his most distinctive adornment, a small skull-cap with brocade of silver, gold, or gemstones, according to its owner's capacity for luxury.

When not working, the Sart likes to drink tea or to amuse himself by singing to the accompaniment of the dutar, a two-stringed folk instrument. Both the melody and the song are improvised, and the lyrics can accordingly be highly eccentric. For example,

16

> My sister is insane.
> She rides on a camel.
> She does not know me . . .

Or, less coherently,

> There comes a man with a white beard.
> He is large . . .

As it is forbidden in the Koran to sing from the chest, the song is delivered in a falsetto voice and ornamented with endless coloratura. This is a typical Arabic style of song, also existing in Spanish flamenco music.

Another highly prized activity is inciting quail cocks to do battle – with fierce gambling and speculation on the outcome. In the pandemonium of the bazaar it is not unusual to see a group of Sarts encircling a pair of fighting quails, following the battle with breathless excitement.

Occasionally a woman passes by, wrapped in the white robes that obscure every line of her figure. Over her face she wears a netted veil of horse-hair which obliterates her features from external view. The veil is taken off only within the confines of the harem, where she lives out a joyless drudging existence, her sole duty to bring sons to the world.

The procedure for finding a wife amongst the Sarts is expensive and largely reduced to a game of chance. The prospective husband sends his mother or sister to select the wife-to-be, who only after the completion of the ceremony takes off her veil and reveals her face. For many, this moment can be nothing but an unpleasant surprise; accordingly, love does not find a mild climate in which to prosper.

A common diversion in the bazaar are the dances of the pubescent *batcha* – the dancing boys. Festooned with jewels, and with faces prettily painted, they go through a set of curiously choreographed movements; the feet stamp out the rhythm while the torso moves playfully from side to side. The faces of the *batcha* are blank and expressionless during performance. They are always surrounded by admiring crowds.

Starving dogs are everywhere, forever trying to steal food. The Sart believes the dog to be an unclean animal – food he will not give it, but kicks, blows and abuse are always forthcoming in plenty. The dogs of the bazaar are usually scrofulous and unhealthy, with skin in soft folds around their sharp bones.

The water-sellers carry their skins on their backs, hawking each cup for a 'tjeka' coin, less than a kopeck. Vagrant groups of dervishes in towering felt hats sing haunting songs, and utter terrible curses at those who do not repond to their begging.

The odours of the multitude of peoples for whom hygiene is an unknown concept blend with the gentle fragrance of saffron and rose oil, the fumes of meat and fish fried in sheep fat, and the stench of bad eggs and rotten fruit. In the alleys of the chicken bazaar, the poultry lies from sunrise to dusk dumped in great piles, legs tied together with twine. In another quarter stand the indigenous sheep of Central Asia, with bulging fatty tails serving the same function as the camel's hump – a larder against the asperity of the desert. From Orenburg comes a breed of sheep whose tails are so bulbous that they drag along the ground. Small wheels are tied beneath to facilitate movement.

In the raisin bazaar, the vendors lord it like kings on top of thrones of fragrant raisins. Here, one does not buy a kilo or two, the heaps of produce must be bought wholesale; black, yellow or brown raisins, each vendor shrieks and proclaims the supremacy of his own pile. The silversmiths, the potters, the tailors and the cobblers each have their own section. Work proceeds without undue haste, and the results are admirable. Leather work far superior to that of Europe. Boots of skin soft as velvet, and ornamented with a delicate and refined beauty.

But the most heavenly thing of all to behold, a compendium of the most diverse colours, is the fruit market. In great circular baskets all the bounty of Nature lies in wait. Up to forty-two different kinds of grape, hanging in rich clusters several feet long – black, yellow, rose-coloured or blue, large as plums, round, oval, opaque or shimmering like wax! Isabel grapes refracting all the colours of the rainbow, Muscat grapes with a scent of honey, and the grapes of Karschi with aroma as heady as perfume.

A riot of peaches, large as children's heads, each filled with a half-pint of creamy juice. Nectarines, figs of yellow, blue and green, honey melons and watermelons so colossal that a single slice of their blood-red flesh would make a very adequate meal. Pomegranates with button seeds, mustard-yellow and shiny red peppers, violet aubergines, scallions and every other conceivable onion, and a similar assortment of regal pumpkins. What scents and colours for eyes and noses long deprived and lips parched with thirst! The very quintessence of the East!

And only a few steps away, outside the lively trade of the bazaar, in deep dust and among the scattered ruins of cenotaphs and ravished blocks of stone, in the glare of merciless sunlight, sit the lepers. They sit immobile with bowed heads, black cloth over their faces. On the ground in front of them, in a silent plea for alms, they keep small wooden bowls. Like dark demons, reminding one of death, they wait while the sun lavishly pours its gold over their misery.

The Russians live in the new suburbs of Samarkand. Also my father had his villa in these parts. Generally, even this area is badly constructed, with architecture inspired partly by the European and partly the Sart influence. Only official buildings boast two or three floors. Life would be unbearable here were it not for the gardens and the tree-lined alleys which throw some shade over the boulevards. On both sides of the streets, water is led through small channels from the Hissar Massif to the city itself. This precious water which irrigates the gardens is shared with Christian virtue amongst the house-owners, although in truth many an enterprising gardener must use the cover of night to flood his garden illicitly.

The Russians have done precious little to install themselves more comfortably in Samarkand. The whole thing looks rather provisional. There are no trams, no street-life to compare with the Old Town. The Sarts work as drivers in dilapidated carriages drawn by skeletal horses more dead than alive. In our part of town there was only one public bath-house and two private bathrooms. One belonged to the governor and the other to my family. Life's necessities were, for the others, relegated to the darkest corners of the gardens.

The winter is mild; if snow should fall it will melt with great timidity at the merest sight of the sun. As do wood anemones in the North, so the white blooms of almond trees herald the coming of spring in the East. February is usually the harbinger. By March, the gardens are in full bloom. Even the mud roof-tops come alive with grasses and flowers; goats and sheep make full use of this fresh grazing. Spring is the most pleasant season in Central Asia, and the evenings especially are filled with reverential wonder. We would often sit on the terrace outside our house and watch the twilight descending; a myriad of frogs held their evensong in the irrigation channels that encircled our land. Somewhere, a Sart would be singing a plaintive song and plucking the strings of his dutar. Above our heads, the whistling wings of Egyptian doves would die away as darkness set in; when the paraffin lamps were lit, great moths with copper-coloured wings came in their hundreds, and sylph-like silver swarmers and bumbling heavy beetles that fell down on the tablecloth with a noisy crash. Slowly the Eastern skies would fill with a multitude of rising stars.

But if spring is a time of beauty then summer in the same measure is a time of unmitigated suffering. It lasts for six months, and in this period not a single drop of rain falls over the thirsting earth. Within a matter of days, everything that was green is toasted, shrivelled, and covered in a thick layer of dust. After midday it is not advisable to go into the open. The air vibrates in the heat as if suspended above a boiling kettle. Man and beast suffer; only dark clouds of flies circle restlessly. Breathing is akin to fire-eating, and there is no lake or other water to cool one's burning body.

The wealthier Russians escape during these months to a hill-station by the River Agalik. Its rapids and rocky waters may prevent swimming, but nevertheless cooler air wafts over the churning waters. Here, these poor Europeans wait out the torturous summer season.

All day the inch-deep dust hangs like a smog over the city and penetrates into the nose, throat and lungs. One's clothes are powdered chalky white. In the evenings shopkeepers and householders sprinkle water from the depleted irrigation channels over the dust, in a vain attempt to bind it. For a few weary hours there is a smell of damp earth, but as soon as the sun rises, their toil is obliterated.

During the dark summer and autumn evenings, I would often wake up to the sound of wailing jackals; if, soon after, the chickens began to fuss, I could be sure that the jackals were investigating the hen-house.

21

As I rushed out I had to prepare myself for the repulsive touch of the big fruit bats that flew with great stealth, and for some reason always against one's face. The screams of jackals and the soft and insipid touch of bats are in my mind inseparable from the memory of dark and starless autumn nights in Samarkand. On one occasion when the aforementioned were sending both me and the chickens into paroxysms of fear, I suddenly stopped dead in my tracks, fascinated by a sudden illumination of the sky. The zodiacal lights flamed across the sky like great spotlights. The screams of the jackals were gone, the bats returned to their hiding holes, and to this young child's imagination, the fire seemed to radiate from a heavenly portal high above the earthly towers of the city of dreams.

4

The Red Ghost

To clarify the events of this story, I must here say a few words about my origins and family.

I am of Byelorussian origins, and was in my early childhood adopted by a Danish family. My adoptive father had in his youth emigrated from Denmark to Russia, where he had married a society lady from St Petersburg. He was, as this story begins, the chairman of the Russo-Asiatic Bank in Samarkand. Also staying with us was my adoptive mother's brother Boris, who had managed to escape the Revolution in Petersburg. He was an officer, a worthy representative of the old Russian aristocracy whose family's endeavours could be traced back to the time of the Crusades. But Boris was an unworldly dreamer who had never been able to summon any real enthusiasm for the soldier's profession, in spite of his popularity among the uncommissioned men. His greatest sorrow was that he had had to leave his mother in St Petersburg when he fled for his life. In Samarkand he wore only civilian clothes, usually one of my father's suits as it was not wise to be seen in an officer's uniform. His one and consuming passion was astronomy, to which he devoted all his spare time and interest: his favourite recreation was purposefully to examine every inch of the fifteenth-century observatory – constructed by the great Tartar chief Ulegh-Begh – which belonged to

23

Samarkand's halcyon days and had only recently been excavated.

My parents had a great many friends; every Thursday a quartet played music in our home. A number of German and Austrian officers, prisoners of war whose internment in Samarkand was more in the nature of an exile, gathered there. Most had married Russian women, and had become almost completely naturalised. Politics was the predominant subject in our conversations; the Great War figured less in our minds than the Revolution. Nobody took the latter very seriously. The general consensus was that Wrangel and Denikin would put down the insurrection in less than two months. Everybody remembered the failed putsch of 1905.

But the red ghost, far from disappearing, became more and more insistent. No derision could make it disappear. In fact, it came closer every day. Samarkand began to change, imperceptibly at first. The soldiers started to behave brashly; general discipline suffered. They came marching arm-in-arm with their girls in drunken legions extending right across the streets. They demonstrated their newly awakened passion for freedom by spitting at everyone they met. Sunflower seeds became effective missiles. Their exuberance often spilled into fighting. No police ever interfered in 'army business'. A nearby shop was plundered in the middle of the day. Still no voice of order made itself heard. A friend of ours came home in nothing but his shirt. He had been detained by a group of armed soldiers who had confiscated his suit. He was glad still to be in possession of his shirt and his life. Finally, with sadness, one avoided the main streets and squares. The customary stillness of the new suburbs changed into constant noise and tension. People stood in groups discussing and shouting each other down. In the public places communist speakers held forth, but their eloquence consisted mainly of endless oaths and threats against the bourgeois system. Their every word was hailed with grateful cries and applause.

One fine day the chief of police was found murdered, and the governor was abducted. After that, things moved quickly. Samarkand declared itself independent, and a new committee was entrusted with running the city. The representatives on the committee were unlikely men, whose functions were amorphous and unspecified. A postman was promoted to minister for education, charged with enlightening the people through new knowledge. A man who normally greased the wheels of trains became minister of communications. Soon the city was cut off, its rail links out of service. The tracks were ripped out by night; the only remaining and serviceable line was to Bokhara; however, this was a forbidden destination, as the Emir of this city had declared its independence, and was regarded as an enemy of the Revolution.

The merely incompetent were just an irritation. As time wore on, it was the craven and the bloodthirsty we worried about. I recall one nineteen-year-old komissar who had made it his speciality to shoot people in the face. With evident satisfaction he aimed his bullet between the eyes of those who had either served in the old regime, or who simply bore well-known or aristocratic names.

Before long the Russo-Asiatic Bank was closed, and my father was without employment. As he anticipated a long stretch of time before any semblance of normality returned, and because he could not endure the nervous strain of doing nothing except waiting for change, he took the bold step of starting up no fewer than four factories. As labourers he engaged the prisoners of war, who were all too pleased to accept the offer. Two of the factories manufactured shoes, a third cigarettes, and the fourth, metal goods, soap and toiletries. All of these were products which had disappeared from daily circulation and could no longer be imported into the stranded city. Only staple products were now available. Thanks to reasonable managerial skills and a co-operative workforce, the factories prospered and, curiously, were able to operate undisturbed for a whole year before coming under the scrutiny of the authorities. 'Controllers' appeared on the scene, and given the evident success of the factories, they soon began to talk of an industrial levy. This was a sure sign that the factories would meet the same fate as every other enterprise in Samarkand – they would be nationalised.

In fact, this did happen after a few months. The authorities took over the running of the factories, a task they performed so badly that before long the whole enterprise collapsed. The prisoners of war were forced to leave their employment after applying in vain for sizeable sums in unpaid wages.

There was still one small grain of hope. We waited for liberation at the hands of Malleson, the English general, camped with his forces in Merw. People even began to learn English so that they could welcome him properly. Soon even this hope was dashed.

Personal lust for power, hate and vengeance now held sway *de facto* in Samarkand; the rulers did not even bother to disguise their violent deeds with the thin veneer of revolutionary ideology. Many of the proponents of the new order could not speak Russian, which was unremarkable as they were often fetched from the itinerant population of prisoners of war. Czechs, Hungarians, Germans and Austrians ruled over Samarkand. But so swiftly did they succeed each other that it was impossible to know who tomorrow would be the abuser of power.

26

One morning I was accosted by a Red Guard in the street outside our garden. He asked me if this were the place where the industrialist lived. Nervously I asked him if anything was wrong. He replied officiously that he had come to collect the industrial tax. He wondered if my father intended to pay with the old Nicolai notes, Kerensky money or Bolshevik roubles. He grinned at me, and, with unexpected candour, added, 'You see, little friend, if your father pays up with the Tsar's roubles then I'll keep them for myself and account for the whole sum with Bolshevik money . . .' This would amount to a neat profit for the canny soldier, unless his superiors were even cleverer than him. The Bolshevik money was printed on such rough paper that after a short time in circulation it was flimsy and useless.

By this time Samarkand had been thoroughly and meticulously plundered. The bazaars had been looted, and most of the Sart merchants ruined. Armed soldiers regularly ventured into the Old Quarter to 'nationalise' whatever goods they pleased. In spite of the introduction of rationing, food supplies gradually dwindled. The bread, mixed with hemp seed and other additives, was almost unfit for human consumption. My father established clandestine links with rich Sarts and Jews, and he succeeded in smuggling in by night the most basic necessities, which were immediately buried in our garden. Thus we had stores of sugar, tea, flour and wine. Jewellery, gold and silver artefacts, and anything else of value, had been similarly concealed for some time since the next ignoble chapter in the Revolution had already begun: house inspections. These, most commonly, occurred at night. No one felt safe.

My father had earned the displeasure of the authorities by pronouncing on several occasions his pride to be a citizen of Denmark – a democratic monarchy. In time, he learned to withold his sentiments, but the error had already been made, and our family came under constant scrutiny. One night we were driven out of our beds by a detachment of Red Guards who sluiced through the house and stole whatever it pleased them to have. Luckily we had been expecting the visit, so there was not much left of real value. Everything had been buried. The raid, however, was followed by many others, until our nerves were quite shattered. At any time one could be awakened by the brutal sound of rifle butts against the front door.

Life was becoming unbearable. Every day brought fresh laws and decrees; and, more disturbingly, a fresh crop of atrocities and murder. Those whose social position in the community had offended the authorities were flung into jail. Genuine criminals were released to make room for the innocent. Bad tidings reached us in a constant trickle. Some of our friends had been imprisoned, others butchered in the street or hanged without trial or sentence.

Passing soldiers amused themselves by firing volleys of rifle shots at our villa, or throwing hand-grenades into the garden. The cow my father had bought to secure our milk supplies was stolen, and our horse and carriage nationalised. No one knew what was happening in Russia; there had been no letters or newspapers for months. The telegraph station had been razed to the ground. To leave the city was forbidden on pain of death. All social interaction was clandestine, and frank discussions were reluctantly embarked upon. No one knew who could be trusted, or who was a spy. Paranoia was the ruling passion. Death would soon be preferable to this inversion of human life. And that my family was on the condemned list was a certainty, impossible to refute.

My father began to make excursions into the Old Town. I asked him why he was away so much, now that his factories had been shut down. He replied evasively, saying that he was having conferences with his friends. Often he brought back gold, silver and jewels in his pockets, and his face became increasingly charged with tension. Finally he took us all into his study, and made sure that all the windows and doors were sealed from any eavesdroppers. He told us the meaning of his visits into the Old Town. For some time he had been preparing for a most desperate and perhaps lethal undertaking: our flight from Samarkand.

5

A Dramatic New Year's Eve

Usually there was a strictly enforced curfew after nine o'clock, but on New Year's Eve 1919 an exception was being made so that the citizens of Samarkand could celebrate the occasion. And, it must be said, the soldiers acted as if they were lunatics released from an asylum. Gunfire crackled at every street-corner. The Red Guards amused themselves by firing into the air, and some contrived to express their joy by throwing hand-grenades. To our hardened ears, the night's explosions were mere expressions of a primitive exuberance.

In my father's old bank, a komissar had established his 'Office of Murder', as it was playfully known. This evening, the soldiers had managed to winch a light-gauge cannon on to a high balcony of the building and from there they discharged barrage after barrage over the town, with gleeful indifference to the odd direct hit on a house. A young woman who had been carousing with the merry gunners protested when a salvo from the cannon demolished a mud house. She was unwise to have voiced her conscience. In less than a second her fickle admirers had hauled her up and flung her over the balcony railings. She fell into the branches of a tree, and from there into a water cistern. This saved her life.

During the course of the year, the well-known director Limantoff from the Moscow National Theatre had come on tour to Samarkand, where he shortly afterwards found himself stranded. To occupy himself he had formed a small theatre company of amateur and professional actors, and with this troupe he performed plays every week. My family had become good friends with Limantoff, and both my mother and I had acted in his play *Before Sunrise*. But as always, the authorities got wind of our activities, which were forbidden at once. In an attempt to boost morale, Limantoff had invited us and other friends to the little theatre where we had previously staged our productions. We had arranged that each of us should bring as much food and beverage as possible, and secondly, that we should dress for the occasion. The object was to forget, for one brief evening, the outside world. A few of the actors among us had promised to sing and recite dramatic pieces. It was to be an escapist evening, an event to be savoured.

Two Austrian officers married to actresses in the troupe had agreed to give us a lift. I remember waiting in the rainy night, listening to the hellish discord from the city, and wondering whether it was really a good idea to go anywhere. But the promise of gaiety and companionship overcame our trepidation, and we set off through fire and whistling bullets. As we passed the Russo-Asiatic Bank, we witnessed the above-mentioned scene on the balcony.

The director and his actors had done their utmost to create a cosy ambience in the modest theatre. On the stage they had put an elegant table decorated with green branches and green silk ribbons – the colour of hope and re-birth. The invited guests unwrapped their parcels and hoarded bottles. Thirty people sat down to dinner. The wind howled around the thin walls, the rain drummed against the metal roof, and everyone talked and laughed with forced vivacity to drown the riotous sounds from

31

outside. We even tried to sing a song. Most of those present were mourning the death or imprisonment of friends and relatives. The meagre hope of our party was to diminish unhappiness for one single night. At the stroke of midnight, Limantoff rose from his chair and lifted his glass. I can still see his face as, with great sobriety and stillness, he said, 'A happy New Year to you all . . .' We were moved by the moment, and sat in silence, dwelling on the thought that this could be our very last New Year. But our solemnity was shattered by a sudden intensification of the barrage. It sounded as if the front of a major battle were just outside. Our supply of wine soon ran dry, and without artificial means it was impossible to sustain a party atmosphere in this inauspicious setting. Whispered prayers came from some of the women. Others crossed themselves; and a few gave vent to tears.

Then came the sound we all knew so well: rifle butts against the front entrance! The doors flew open with a great crash and in marched a ragged band of drunken soldiers, wet as dogs and armed to the teeth with hand-grenades and rifles. With one swift movement we all jumped to our feet and stood as if nailed to the floor. Our tormentors' muddy eyes were full of hate; they growled and stumbled their way through the rows of benches until they stood below the stage; some took aim at us with their rifles, while others weighed hand-grenades in their unsteady hands.

'I see . . . here we have the *burschuj* [the bourgeoisie] of the city,' their leader screamed. He was a fanatical type with long hair, beard stubble several days old, and wild bloodshot eyes. 'Damn you devils! Bloodsuckers! For three hundred years you've sucked the blood out of us, but now your time has come at last . . .' He shook his grenade at us. We hardly dared breathe. 'Damned *burschuj* . . . now you're going to hell all at the same time!' Limantoff was the first of us to get his voice back. 'Wait, comrade,' he cried, trying to make his voice as firm as possible. 'We're no *burschuj*, we're penniless actors.'

'Actors!' the soldiers echoed, both with disbelief and delight.

'Prove it, you bastards,' shouted the threadbare commander, detecting a slight diminishment of his authority. 'Play for us, and then we'll see if you're actors or not . . .'

'Yeah, play for us . . . play for us!' his compatriots bawled drunkenly; and they took to their seats and slammed their muddy boots against the velour of the seats in front.

'Get going, will you, or we'll shoot you one by one, like sparrows, understand?' To emphasise his words, the speaker blasted a salvo into the ceiling. The plaster came raining down over the parquet flooring of the stage to great cheers of approbation from the stalls.

The director gave the order to the pianist, and called for the company's comic to perform an impromptu song. But the leader sprang to his feet and bellowed, 'Oh no you don't, you vermin . . . first you'll play the Internationale, and you others,' he added, shaking his fist at us, 'you'll sing along, you damned canaries, and if there's so much as one of you that doesn't sing, I'll open your mouths with this . . .' And once again he showed us his hand–grenade. Evidently he was furious not to have already despatched us. The pianist launched into the Internationale, which for most of us was an unknown song. It was the first time I had ever heard it. Its notes etched themselves into my childish memory. Even today when I hear it, I am filled with a panicked anguish. There was little or no fighting spirit in our rendition of the anthem. Those of us who did not know the song mimed with our pale lips as well as

33

we could. We sang for our lives, while an intoxicated soldier stamped out the rhythm with his great boot. The others with hiccups and belching initiated a running commentary on our faces and clothes. A few of the freedom fighters were leaning over the backs of the front-row chairs, retching on to the floor.

'. . . who carry the people's joy . . .' At last we concluded the verse. The comic was allowed on stage, and he performed a few of the popular pieces in his repertoire. These were a great success, and the atmosphere improved by several degrees. Next, there were calls for 'girls' from the pit, and we tried to persuade the primadonna to recite something for the men. Our efforts were wasted on her. She steadfastly refused. Once again, the tension became oppressive.

'For fuck's sake, are we going to get any theatre? Or would you rather have a blast from this? Give us that whore, we're going to tickle her!'

This was too much for the young and beautiful primadonna. With flaming eyes she rushed forward and, trembling with hatred, cried, 'You damned swine!' Immediately, and with great presence of mind, Limantoff gave her such a shove that she tumbled into the wings, out of sight. This saved her life, for one of the soldiers had already taken aim at her.

'On with the programme,' roared the commander. 'We want some dancing . . .'

'Yeah, dance for us, dance for us,' cried his mindless underlings.

'We're not dancers,' Limantoff corrected. 'We're actors . . .'

'Wait a little while,' came a voice from the prompt-box, where evidently someone was concealed. The voice was that of a young girl who had been taken on as an apprentice at the theatre. Her father was a rich merchant who had been imprisoned six months before. Limantoff helped her on to the boards.

'I shall dance for you all,' she called with a disarming smile for our audience. 'As long as you promise to leave when I have finished . . .'

'Just get going, will you, so we can get it over and done with . . . or do you think we want to sit here gawping at you all night?' came the witty reply.

With great bravado, the pianist hammered out the first bars of a folk melody; he played with such fury that the whole piano shook. For a moment, the girl stood with clenched teeth, her eyes filled with tears.

'Fortissimo, fortissimo,' she cried, and the pianist lunged desperately at his keys. And then she started to dance. I have seen many dances since that night, but never performed with such fury. So intensely did she move across the stage that her skirts stood like a ring around her hips; her hair shook free and tumbled down over her shoulders, while pins and brooches fell and bounced over the stage. She kicked her feet high above her head, and her arms flailed as if she had wings. The tears were running over her face and she was singing with a breathless voice. Wider and wider she ranged, in ever-more frenzied motions. We had to withdraw into the wings to give her space. The soldiers were bawling their approval of her and her underwear. The performance finished with a hysterical attack – she fell to the ground, and started to convulse and scream. The soldiers, who considered this to be a fine and proper climax, broke into spontaneous applause.

'More dancing if you please, more dancing,' they ordered. The pianist played a weary waltz, to which we all danced in uneasy couples. I don't suppose that I shall ever dance a more dramatic *valse macabre*. The acclamation from below became riotous. An empty bottle of vodka shattered against the piano so that glass

35

splinters whirled about our feet. The dancing faltered, but when we looked up, our tormentors were on their way out with loud whoops and jeers. As a farewell gesture, they let off a few rounds into the ceiling, and then disappeared in a hail of falling plaster. Once outside, they threw a hand-grenade which detonated in the park.

My legs were shaking, my hands were cold as ice, my throat felt so curiously dry. All I wanted to do was weep. Once we had braved the hostile city and were safely home, that is exactly what I did, and my mother too. None of us could sleep. Father, Mother, Boris and I sat around the table in the dining room, smoking cigarettes and drinking wine. That was the first cigarette I ever smoked. The wine made me feel heavy, and so I fell asleep with my cheek against the tear-drenched table-top. As I fell into unconsciousness, I heard the mumuring of the adults' voices, discussing and planning the one thing that seemed to have any significance – our flight, our desperate flight!

6

A Birthday Surprise Party

I was destined to have the pleasure of one more party, which in terms of dramatic surprise would even outshine the previous one.

It was my birthday in February, and my parents had decided to use it as a pretext for gathering our friends together one last time. No one in our aquaintance had the slightest idea about our escape plans. To have the slenderest chance of success, they had to be kept entirely secret. Eighteen people were invited. In honour of the day we had dug up our silver cutlery and candlesticks, and the table looked festive when we sat down extra early at six o'clock to have supper – for already by the nine o'clock curfew our guests had to back in their homes.

Everyone had come, except a Swedish lady from Gothenburg; Fru Bent was married to a Danish artist, but these days she had to earn her own living by offering Swedish massage. An hour before the party she had been called to the house of a komissar, but she had promised to join us as soon as she could. Our maid was just beginning to serve the delicious bortsch soup when the door-bell rang. I ran into the hall. Obviously this was our belated guest! I did not even bother to ask who it was, a precaution one always employed before opening the door, especially after dark.

Quick as a flash, a bayonet was pushed through the

crack, and held with some menace against my stomach. I screamed with all the might of my twelve-year-old lungs. The guests came rushing into the hall. A soldier shoved me out of the way with his bayonet and stepped inside, followed by three henchmen. All four were drunk, armed with rifles, revolvers and bayonets and criss-crossed with ammunition belts. They were wearing the Bolshevik uniform – leather jackets and caps emblazoned with the red star of the Soviet.

'Hands up! Stand still, *burschuj!*' came the order. We raised our hands as they uncocked their guns. It would be an exaggeration to say that any of us were particularly frightened. Guns were part of the daily routine; it was almost impossible to go out without being subjected to a frisking. But we realised after a few moments that this was no ordinary house inspection – when such raids were carried out in the name of 'the state', the soldiers were required to show their warrants and identification papers. We had fallen into the hands of what was simply a band of robbers. It was yet another new experience for me. Our lives were hanging on a thread which, if possible, had become even thinner and finer than before.

The spokesman for the band was a typical Armenian with blue-black hair, thick eyebrows, dark brown skin and bulbous lips. He had the physiognomy of a true criminal. He stepped forward, gloating at the effect of his entrance. Fingering his Browning, he made a half-bow, and in a mockingly servile voice said, 'Begging you pardon, ladies and gentlemen. I am deeply sorry that we are disturbing your charming party, but duty comes before everything, as you know. I am a revolutionary commissioner . . .'

'Does that mean you have to ambush us like this?' my father demanded forcefully.

'Shut up!' the Armenian shouted. 'Who's the host

here?' The question verified our suspicions that they had picked our house randomly and were entirely unauthorised.

'I am the host,' my father said. The Armenian walked up to him, shoved his face up close and stared insolently into his eyes; but my father was unimpressed, more repelled than anything else by the stench of vodka which perfumed each odious word.

'I am here to conduct a search of this house. If anyone moves, he's dead! And there's no point trying to escape, I've got the whole place surrounded by soldiers. Get on with it!' He positioned one soldier to the left, and one to the right of the door. The fourth was stationed in the salon. While they were organising themselves, there came a dull thud as one of our guests, the young daughter of the sacked district attorney, collapsed on the floor. Her fiancé, a Czech prisoner of war called Bondy, rushed forward to assist her. He stopped when he felt the cold steel of a revolver against his forehead.

'Don't you move an inch . . .' shouted the guard. The poor girl remained in a pale and motionless swoon.

'May I help her?' my mother asked.

'Charity starts at home, you old bag,' screamed the Armenian, 'make one move and I'll mow you down like a whore . . . !' Thereafter he commanded us to sit down on a Turkish sofa in a corner of a room.

'All of you,' he insisted with a movement of the revolver. Obligingly we pressed ourselves into the sofa, and as there were almost twenty of us, confusion set in as we climbed over each other; but the situation was, in spite of its absurdity, far from comical.

'You scum! If we find any weapons on your persons we'll shoot you like dogs . . .'

'No one here is carrying a weapon,' my father assured him.

'Search them!' ordered the Armenian. The man at the

39

door leaned his rifle against the wall, and proceeded to frisk my father. He seemed far from experienced at this, for his hands slid timidly over the pockets. Besides, his stupor made him almost insensible to what he was doing. This, as we shall see, was extremely fortuitous.

Bondy, whose turn it was next, received a painful knock on the head from a revolver when he failed immediately to understand the Armenian's order to remove his overcoat. The ladies, whose screams seemed to give immense pleasure to our tormentors, soon kept indignant silence again.

I had the honour of being the third person to be searched, but they netted only an indiarubber from my trouser pocket. My shoes were scrutinised with particular interest, as if it were likely that I would keep a revolver in a toe-cap!

Suddenly we heard a voice from outside, in the porch. Apparently it was the leader of the band, who preferred to remain unseen.

'Shoot the bastards! What are you waiting for? Send them packing! Haven't we had enough of this rabble? Why these damned Chinese ceremonies, eh? Take those swine and put out their eyes with your bayonets, you idiots! Parasites! We're going to hunt you down until you're extinct, every one of you!' He was holding forth as if he were clinically insane, and he had an unusually fruity store of curses.

The search continued, while the women looked on impotently. If one of us had been carrying a gun, then without a doubt there would have been bloodshed. Boris's pipe trembled so violently between his teeth that in the end he dropped it on the floor; but when he reached down to pick it up, one of the guards immediately took aim at him. After that, we all froze.

The Armenian noticed our maid, who was standing

quite terrified in the doorway and staring at the spectacle. He bowed to her with extravagant courtesy and spoke gallantly: 'Good evening, fair comrade. Please, come inside! Won't you sit down? You're a proletarian, there's no need for you to stand up while these swine are sitting down. They should stand up, and you rest your feet!' He fetched a chair for her, but she rushed back to the kitchen and told the staff what was happening in the salon. The cook had experienced similar adventures on numerous occasions and he did not bother to come and see for himself. Had he done so, we could have alerted him in German to the danger of our situation amongst these cut-throats.

While all this was going on, I was standing next to my father; to reassure myself, I slipped my hand into his, which he held against his back. I wanted him to know that I was there, and that I certainly was not frightened. Immediately, he entrusted me with a heavy emerald ring which he had kept hidden. Unnoticed, I tucked it inside my shirt. To give him the sign that all was well, I gave him my hand once again, and this time I felt a thick roll of money. Bondy who had recovered after the blow to his head, saw what we were doing; to assist us in our perilous sleight of hand, he distracted the guards by making a movement towards his fiancée, who was beginning to stir.

'Halt . . . you,' the guard said, with a menacing movement. In that moment I slipped the money into my Russian blouse. Forty-five thousand roubles, a sizeable roll of money, rested against my belt in the folds that I hastily arranged to make it invisible. By now, all the men had been searched, and the Armenian, with a sleazy smile, made a new decree.

'The ladies must be examined *en cabinet séparé*,' he announced, and opened the door to my bedroom. The women were ushered in before him, and having ordered

41

the soldiers to guard us well, he went inside and closed the door. I will not even bother to relate his behaviour towards the women while he searched through their hair, corsets and stockings. The waiting husbands in the salon clenched their fists in futile agony. They could do nothing. The slightest effort to assist their wives would have resulted in a fatal bullet. At last the door re-opened and the women were shoved back into the sofa.

The girl who had fainted was crying hysterically, having woken up to an unpleasant reality from the dreamless swoon. Bondy was trying to calm her. The Armenian grabbed my mother and, with an armed escort on her other side, forced her to accompany him through the house. In the dining room, the partially served food was still on the table. The guard gawped at the unusual sight of a European table service. He picked up a silver spoon, thrilled at its weight and lustre. Greedily, he stared at the cutlery around the table.

'Is this real silver?' he asked my mother, but before she could answer the Armenian interrupted.

'Put that spoon back . . . we're not robbers, are we?'

Evidently, he had decided to continue with his ploy of being a legitimate official in the employ of the state; 'confiscating' money and arms was the norm, but if *objets d'art* were taken, it could lead to complications. The other soldier, however, did not believe in such niceties, for he pocketed a gold wrist-watch which Bondy had left on an upstairs sideboard. The wardrobes caused a frenzy of interest. They flung the clothes into a pile on the floor. My mother later told me that she had almost passed out with suspense.

Bondy, it turned out, had given her with a small pouch of a thousand roubles in gold coins, which she had hidden on a hanger under a dress; because the robbers were tossing out the contents of the wardrobes indiscriminately, the coins fell silently against the soft

42

linen on the floor. Bondy, in the next room, could hear what was happening in the bedchamber, and his teeth were chattering with anguish. The money represented freedom for this prisoner of war and his young fiancée. The guard was intoxicated by all the fine silk hosiery and gowns. He shoved his nose into armfuls of clothes, sniffing at the delicate scents.

'Ah, this shall be mine . . . and this . . . and this . . .,' He scrambled like a madman amongst the garments while my mother waited apprehensively for him to find the pouch of gold. Once again, the Armenian saved the day by repeating his noble sentiment. 'We're not robbers, for Christ's sake. Leave the old bag's dresses! What do you think we are, simple thieves?' And the answer to this question, we all reflected, had to go begging. When they had at last rummaged through all the boxes and cupboards, torn down the curtains, stuck their bayonets through mattresses and toppled furniture, the two men returned with my mother to the salon, where the rest of us were still being guarded.

The Armenian grabbed my father by the scruff of his neck and pulled him out of the sofa.

'Where is the money?'

'I don't have any money . . .'

'Don't talk like that . . . I know you're rich . . . you used to own the factories. Well, didn't you?'

'Yes, maybe I used to own a factory or two, but they've all been closed down . . .'

'You're lying, you thieving dog! Give me the money, or I'll put a bullet through your head right now!'

'I'm a Danish citizen.'

'I don't care what you are, understand? You give me money or I'll put a bullet . . .'

Standing there and watching my father, I felt the roll of money burning against my skin. Should I hand it over? My hand began to move towards the buttons of my Russian blouse. The voice from outside came back with redoubled strength: 'If they won't part with their roubles then just cut their guts open . . . let them pay with their entrails.' This last threat decided me, but before I could act, the doorbell rang.

The invisible man must have dealt with the visitor, for we heard him hissing, 'House search, if you please . . .' The outer door was slammed in her face, but we had all recognised Fru Bent's voice. Evidently she had managed to slip through the alleged cordon of soldiers round the house, which meant that there was no escort; this being the case, she must have realised that unauthorised men were holding us up. Perhaps at this very minute she was heading for the nearest militia office. The invisible man must have come to the same conclusion, for he started to yell from the porch that we should all be butchered without further delay. Then there was silence. The Armenian began to look a little insecure, but he pulled himself up, and fixed his eyes on my father.

'For the last time – where is your money?'

'I don't have any . . .'

'Right then! You'll have to accompany me to the fortress.' He knew that the merest mention of the fortress would make us sick with fear. No one ever returned from there. In spite of our certainty that these proletarians were freebooters, we knew that if my father were taken away, it would be a simple thing for them to kill him in some lonely, dark place. My anxiety disappeared, and I went up to the Armenian and pleaded with him.

'Oh sir, kind comrade and komissar, today is my birthday. Could you not possibly allow my father to stay at home?' My father was already putting on his raincoat. The Armenian threw him a thoughtful look, and then looked at me with some confusion. I do not

44

believe that my childish words softened his resolve, but perhaps he pretended to give in to me, so that he could retreat gracefully from the fiasco.

'All right then,' he said to my father, 'you can stay here for now, just because it's your son's birthday. But . . . one thing I'll tell you . . . and that's for sure . . . tomorrow we're coming for you . . . damned *burschuj*!' With this he nodded at his men, and they marched out of the house.

In Samarkand there is a proverb: 'The clay pot will go to the well until the day it breaks . . .' These robbers, it seems, had had their teeth blooded by such nightly forays, and they had become increasingly bold. But one night in March, they had the misfortune of breaking into the house of a council representative and they were arrested at once. The very next morning they were hanged without trial, in the company of an old general and the owner of a cinema. The news of this execution, however, gave us less pleasure than their departure from our home. And the collective exuberance was soon dampened by that strange fit of exhaustion which always follows on the heels of nervous strain.

When finally the birthday cake was brought in, and I puffed at the twelve fluttering candles of my brief life, there was no joy in the listless faces around the table. That was my last Russian birthday party – if party it could even be called.

7

Departure

The days were characterised by a constant anxiety, given additional urgency by the groundless rumours that were circulated, whispered into avid ears and quickly passed on. Malleson, Denikin and Wrangel were taking turns to march on Samarkand with a view to liberating us and flinging the Bolsheviks into the dust. But daybreak usually brought fresh contradictory news, namely that Bolshevik power was growing with the speed of a pestilence, over-running Afghanistan. From Kagan came a fresh crop of rumours, and from Bokhara, and from Kasalinsk too, each batch of facts obliterating its predecessors, until no one knew what to think. Perhaps the wisest course was not to think at all.

And so at last my father brought us the word that we had been waiting for. The day of our escape had been set. We were to leave at Easter – after the rainy season – preferably on Palm Sunday, when every guard in the district would be drunk. Three long months lay ahead of us until this date, but if we had held out for a year and a half, as my father judiciously pointed out, we could surely survive another three months! Our first priority was to reach Bokhara, either through the Hissar or the Tianschan mountains. From Bokhara we hoped to continue by railway, if communications were still under White control. Never before had I longed so much for Easter; no twelve-year-old can ever have counted the days so piously as I did. My father's visits to the Old Quarter became more frequent, and for the first time he received callers at our house. They were mostly Sarts or Bokhara Jews, secretive people whom he took into his study. I caught fragments of muttered conversations regarding routes through mountain passes, desert caravans, camels, horses and ransom money.

One evening my father came home with a man who cut a strange figure: a Sart dressed in ripped boots, a soiled kaftan and a most ignoble turban, but with an imposing full beard dyed red with henna. His name was Salmat-Aka, formerly of immense wealth but now ruined. His father, Salmat the Elder, owned the greatest herds of sheep in Afghanistan.

These two Sarts had once caused a sensation in my father's bank. Salmat the Elder, accompanied by his son and dressed in rags worthy of a beggar, had come into the bank and waited humbly at the counter, wishing to speak to the manager. When my father emerged from the offices, Salmat the Elder asked about the bank's interest rates on saved capital. My father, greatly surprised at the beggar's questions, replied that it depended on the size of the deposit. The old one took a step back and lifted the hem of his garment on to the counter. Inside the lining of his threadbare kaftan he had 760,000 roubles which he had carried from the Old Town – a walk of some two hours.

Now his son, Salmat-Aka, complained bitterly about the loss of the money, and begged my father to reoccupy the bank when times became more stable. It was impossible to explain to Salmat-Aka what these new times augured. All one could do was to sympathise and promise to do one's best. In return, Salmat-Aka undertook to find us a guide who could take us through the Chinese mountains along routes known to few Russians.

47

A few days afterwards a Sart stood outside our gate with a couple of riding horses. We all had to learn to ride, for none among us – Boris excepted – had ever sat on a horse. Boris had soon taught us the rudiments of a good posture and control of the reins. Only my mother seemed unsuited to equestrian pursuits. She weighed almost two hundred pounds, and was a lady of the old Russian style. It was a remarkable thing to see her astride a boisterous mount as it bolted into the far distance. Usually she was rescued by some attentive Sart. She endured her riding lessons with innate humour and commendable stoicism, and these qualities outweighed her lack of talent in the saddle. To those friends who expressed curiosity about our sudden interest in horses, we responded that we were preparing for an Easter excursion to the Agalik and the mountains as soon as the spring rains had ceased.

But the rains seemed interminable to us, consumed as we were by impatience. Every morning I jumped out of bed and ran to the window, but I was forever disappointed by the water pouring out of the open portals of the sky. The water-courses, having filled the canals, were overflowing on to the roads. Deep mud made even the main thoroughfares impassable. In the Old Town, several buildings had been washed away. People stepping gingerly into puddles might plummet up to their necks. Pavements were a rarity and a luxury not seen for many weeks. It was an uncommonly dismal spring. There were mutterings that its like had not been seen in eighty years. Would the benevolent sun never return, dry out the roads, and make them passable to traffic? And the weeping skies, would they be forever hanging over the unhappy city of Samarkand?

At times, events conspired to make us forget about our woes. One day, for instance, there was a soldier in the garden, ordering my father to present himself immediately before the chief komissar. We were paralysed with anticipation, fearing that our escape plans had been discovered.

My father was taken to what used to be the officers' club. Armed soldiers were guarding the entrance. At the long end of the old reading rooms, a rostrum had been erected, and from this elevated position the chief komissar gazed out at the world, surrounded by functionaries. He fixed my father with a triumphant gaze.

'I see that you've been doing a bit of business with the Emir of Bokhara . . . and to deny it would be less than useless. You have delivered a munitions machine. Just plead guilty to this charge . . . we do not like delays . . .'

'But I have never manufactured such equipment,' my father protested. 'One needs very heavy machinery, and certainly more resources than I could ever muster . . .'

'Oh, that is interesting, because we have information proving that you assembled pistols in those same factories . . .'

'Pistols! Did your teams ever inspect my factories? Do you realise what minimal resources I had? I would not have been able to manufacture any pistols.'

'Don't try your tricks on us. We have discovered documentation at the factory, and a receipt from the Emir of Bokhara which beyond doubt proves that he received a machine from you through one of your agents.'

'Yes, that is correct,' my father responded. 'I did deliver a machine for the minting works of the Emir.'

The chief komissar slammed his fist into the table, so that books and documents leapt into the air. 'Don't try to pull the wool over my eyes! How are you ever going to prove to my satisfaction that you delivered nothing but a machine for the Emir's minting operation?' My father, who had a small gold coin from the Emir's

49

machine threaded on to his watch-chain, held it up for examination. Consensus was reached, but the komissar was not quite satisfied.

'Well, what about the guns which are also set down here in your accounts? One day we have 8000 pistols, and the next day 5000 of them. What are you scheming? Is this part of some plot to arm the whole of Bokhara, Afghanistan and Persia with handguns?'

'Where does it say that I supplied pistols?' my father insisted.

'Here,' answered the komissar, and with a triumphant smile he casually flung the accounts book towards my father. He, having seen the relevant entry, found it difficult to suppress a smile.

'Your Eminence, here it says *festoler* not *pistoler*. *Festoler* are small eyelets through which shoelaces are threaded. And I can willingly confirm that these I did manufacture, using a sizeable stamping machine. But I regret to tell you it would have fallen well short of the sort of hardware they have in armament factories . . .'

The komissar and his aides looked distinctly uncomfortable, until the former summoned his wits enough to bash the table once more with a clenched fist.

'Whenever we get further proof of your treasonable activities, we shall simply put you against a wall – do you understand me, you damnable *burschuj*! Now get out of here!' This incident, for all its potential danger, enlivened our morose days for quite some time. My father, meanwhile, had received information that five horses were waiting for us in a nearby village, in the stables of a relative of Salmat-Aka. All but one were for us; the fifth would carry our guide. From Samarkand we would set off in a covered wagon, on the trip that we had openly advertised to our acquaintances. Preferably on Easter night itself, we would continue from the village, hoping that all the sentries would be drunk

50

and incapacitated. Travelling through the mountains, we had a fair chance of reaching the border to Bokhara by morning. This city was itself in imminent danger of falling under the Bolshevik yolk and thus crushing our hopes and cementing our destinies in blood. It was a question of not wasting another moment.

Two days before Easter, the sun deigned to show its bright face. On the following day it shone from dawn to dusk, and repeated its virtuoso performance on Easter Day itself. The roads were drying out, much to our satisfaction; soon the going was passable for an *arba* – that is, a wagon with two colossal wheels.

And then came a morning that I have never forgotten. The sun was radiant on Easter Day, 22 April 1919. At eight o'clock the *arba* was brought out. All portable valuables and jewels had been distributed in four packs; everything else was buried in the garden. Our possessions in the villa were untouched. Nothing had been moved. On the polished sideboard stood the silver bowls and candelabras. Every ornament had to be sacrificed and left behind in the interests of secrecy. We would only be gone for three days, my father had announced to all and sundry. But to his best friend he had confided the true purpose of our excursion, and handed an envelope with three months of salaries for our servants. As my mother climbed into the *arba*, she asked the cook to make certain that fresh bread was available on our return the following Saturday. The maid was to scour the floor and polish the windows. Our gardener, an Austrian by name of Fritz, was told to dig around the peach and apricot trees. When he shook our hands in farewell, he allowed himself a knowing wink. He, alone of all the staff, had an inkling of our true intentions. Thereafter we crawled under the wickerwork screen which covered our *arba*. Our feelings were clear. There was no sorrow at leaving

51

our paradisal garden, no remorse in departing from our beloved home. Such anguish and fear had possessed us these last few months that sentimentality could find no soil for its roots in our dried-up hearts. Already, the anticipation of this huge adventure was heavy on our shoulders, rendering us speechless.

The cart started moving. Our four dogs jumped and pranced around the wheels, and the most loyal of them howled despairingly, as if he knew that he was losing his master and mistress. No one paid any attention to our vehicle. Half an hour later we were driving past the last mud huts of the suburbs. Soon I could see the minarets in the distance behind us, their blue pillars tall and graceful against the cloudless sky which seemed to rest against their glittering domes.

That was the last time I saw the city of my birth.

8

Along the Abyss

Our cart rolled along the road, past mud huts with gardens fresh and green after the long rain. We were huddled as far back as possible so that we could not be seen from the road. Anxious thoughts and the slow tedious rattle of wheels did not lift our spirits. The day passed tardily; at four o'clock we rolled into the farm where another driver should have been awaiting us. A Sart in a blue kaftan and white turban stood politely bowing, greeting us with a few words of Russian awkwardly pronounced. The *arba*, having discharged its passengers, turned around for Samarkand. We dragged our belongings into the garden. Our host spread out a rug under an apricot tree, left us the Turki clothes ordered by my father, and then disappeared into his hut.

Dressed in the indigenous clothes, we stretched out on the soft pillows in the shade. However, our well-being soon turned into alarm as the hours passed with no sign of the driver. My father went several times to make enquiries, but our host would give him no clear assurances. Dusk fell at nine o'clock, and night came. Darkness dropped as a curtain from the sky. We could no longer see each other's faces. Desperately, we tried to invoke some courage. My mother took my hand whilst my father whispered hopefully that the Sart driver was simply waiting for night proper. We had waited for seven hours, and we whispered in the deathly still night just for the pleasure of hearing the sound of other human voices.

At last there was a faint light. It came from a little paraffin lamp in the hand of the Sart with the white turban. In his broken Russian he whispered anxiously: 'Food is coming. Pilau is coming. The driver is coming . . .'

'What sort of driver is he?' asked my father.

'Big man, dangerous man. Not cheap, much money pays him. Have you revolver? Revolver – bang?'

Only one thing seemed of importance, and that was his promise of food; our own supplies were not accessible in the darkness. After another half-hour, he reappeared with bread and a great dish of pilau, a Sart dish of rice and lamb. We tore at it with our fingers as best we could.

Suddenly a second man loomed out of the darkness. He was a stocky and dark-hued Sart in a red turban, carrying a big samovar of tea. He threw himself down on the rug without honouring us with the slightest greeting. Our host sat down next to him, and both these turban-wearing men drank tea from tiny cups without handles, while we steadily ate our pilau. My father examined the Sart gentlemen with a displeased and suspicious countenance, and then he spoke to us casually, in French. 'They don't look particularly reliable. And it's not tea they're drinking, but wine. Don't eat the food, it could well be poisoned!'

At once, the rice aquired a bitter taste, and we regretfully spat it out, turning our attention to the bread. It soon became evident that they were indeed drinking wine. At every cup, they became more unabashed. When we asked if we should not leave soon, they answered with wide, toothless grins. At length their false samovar was emptied of its last drop. The white turban nodded at his red counterpart, and said to my father 'This man shall have a thousand roubles . . .'

'May I ask why?'

'If he not a thousand roubles gets, he shall not show path over mountains. Dangerous mountains. A thousand roubles shall take away the danger . . .'

There was nothing else for it. Father produced a thousand-rouble note and handed it to the red turban. We were ushered through a gate in the garden wall. Five saddled horses, tacked up with saddle bags, were waiting for us. We stowed our luggage. Amongst our more valuable supplies were ten small bags, each weighing a kilo, filled with Imperial Russian silver coins amassed by my father during his visits to the Old Quarter.

In addition, I had brought with me the dearest thing I owned, an intricate English quilt of padded silk, which had been impossible to leave behind. I slung it over the saddle. The red turban rode at the head of the group, followed by the white one, my father, mother, Boris, and I last of them all. However, after a while I become conscious of someone behind me, keeping his distance. We rode at speed. My father, ever solicitous about my mother's welfare, asked if she felt comfortable. At once, the white turban reined in his horse and showered abuse over us for daring to speak. As this Sart was anxious, unstable and drunk, it would have been most unwise to respond to him. While he was transmitting his sinister blend of Sart and Russian oaths, my father turned to me and said, with great possession, 'Don't you be afraid, my boy. Boris and I are riding with our Brownings in our hands. If anyone touches you, just shout . . .'

We started moving again. Worried about the mysterious rider behind me, I swivelled in my saddle continuously. Suddenly my horse slid into a waterlogged ditch, and I lost touch with the other riders. I felt my boots fill with water. After much violent tugging at the reins, I managed to get back on firm ground. Somewhere in the darkness I heard my father.

'Stop! Can you see me?'

'No,' I cried.

'Give me your hand . . .'

I did so, and felt his strong hand. Our horses stood quietly next to each other. Boris and my mother had disappeared. We listened for the sound of plunging hooves, but all we could hear were the leaves rustling in the treetops above us. Then, to our great relief, we heard Boris calling and, soon after, my mother's voice; her horse had been tempted by the water in the same place where I had slid down. Bending its neck to take a drink, it had deposited her unceremoniously in the pool. She was drenched up to her neck.

The path seemed to brighten, and I discovered that we were riding along a dried-up riverbed. For interminable hours we zigzagged through this terrain. My English quilt was lost, but I did not dare even suggest that our Sart driver should stop. The white and the red turbans were whipping their horses as if every Bolshevik in Russia were on their heels. A more potent danger, however, was in unexpected meetings with country-men; with time-honoured Sart jealousy, our guides would then have been reported to the authorities, and deprived of the sizeable profit this expedition would generate. We did pass a few riders, but their greetings went unanswered so that our accents would not give us away.

After midnight, our ponies stopped by a steep incline. The man in the red turban took his farewell and rode off over a nearby bridge. The white turban pointed at the bridge. 'Ten robbers wait under that bridge. One thousand roubles already paid, therefore no danger . . .' Then, pointing at the mountains, he spurred his horse.

There was no obvious way of ascending this slope. It merged with the darkness of the sky. Evidently this was the route recommended by Salmat-Aka, the route not known by Russians. I too put the spurs into my horse, and it leapt forward. Boris and my father were already far ahead.

The ponies were in an almost vertical position, and it was tricky to stay in the saddle. This was particularly serious for my mother, who slid down the rump of her mount time and time again, ending up ignominiously on the stony ground. She persevered, but in the end we had to help her into the saddle of the white turban, so that she could hang on to his back. Even this was futile. Soaked to the skin and exhausted, for three hours she clambered and crawled on all fours. She stumbled between great rocks, slipped on gravel and patches of dew-soaked grass, and lay in despair as floods of sharp stones trickled down the abyss. She, as much as the rest of us, was tortured by an all-consuming thirst. We did not possess a drop of water between us. Towards the end she was weeping; one by one, we dismounted, propped her up, tried to encourage her. Finally I got a proper look at the 'mysterious rider'. He was an old man with grey beard-stubble on his chin. No one knew why he was travelling with us, and no one made any enquiries. He walked beside my mother, sharing her Via Dolorosa, patting her hands in a fatherly way, and muttering empathetic words whose meaning she did not understand.

At last we reached the top of the pass, and my mother fell down half-crazy with tiredness. From our vantage point we could see the moon bathing the land in cool, pale light. Deep below us in the valley the river coiled like a band of silver, and a village shone white. The air was crystal clear. We could see the bridge of the ten robbers. After a short rest, we had to continue.

Every hour was precious. Happily, the path was now more or less level, and my mother could mount her pony. On our left was a vertical rock-face; the path, less than a metre wide, coiled along a ravine several hundred metres deep. Nervously we hugged the side of the rock-face.

'Look to the left, to the left . . .' our driver cried. His terror had rendered him sober. 'To the left, or we are all dead . . .'

Our horses had a slightly better time of it, for they were blindfolded. It was a question of steering them well. Step by step they felt their way forward; they must surely have sensed the mortal danger. Occasionally, a big obstructing rock on the path had to be negotiated, step by step – one wrong-footing could have resulted in a headlong plunge. The path was so narrow that my elbow often scraped against the rock-wall on the left. In spite of the excitement and the imminent danger, I had to exert all my energy to stop myself from falling asleep. I sat in half-slumber, holding my horse's mane in a tight grip, while the stars performed a strange dance before my eyes. It is almost twenty years since I rode along like this under the shadow of death, and still I wake up bathed in sweat, for the memory of this ride will never leave me. We had no idea of our altitude – that is, until we met with great fields of snow so thick that the horses had torturously to wade through it. The wind was like a knife, my bones were frozen; in the east the sky was beginning to flush, casting a purple sheen over the snow; in the west, the moon and stars lost their brilliance.

I spurred my horse, rode up to my father, and said, with as much heroism as my twelve years permitted, 'I am not at all tired. As soon as the sun has risen I will feel completely awake.'

The guide pulled his horse up and whispered, in

faultless Russian, 'Shut up and don't talk rubbish . . .
just be quiet . . .'

'What difference can it possibly make if we say a few
words up here?' objected my father

'Hold your tongue! Many robbers up here are sleeping, but they can easily be aroused. Do not talk . . .'

It would have been interesting to learn what sort
of robber would be sleeping in the snowfields of the
Hissar Mountains at 1,400 metres above sea-level, but
we had no energy for arguments. The white turban was
conscious of his power over us: he was the only one
who could lead us to safety, and we were completely in
his indifferent hands. This was an exquisite, rapturous
feeling for an Oriental.

The sun rose at five in the morning, and shone over
this Easter Monday. We had been in the saddle for nine
hours. When the first rays of light struck my mother,
she stopped her horse and moaned pitifully, 'I must
have water . . .' My father helped her dismount. We
discovered a spring at whose rim sat a toad as large as
a baby's head, staring at us truculently. We fell to our
knees and stilled our thirst. I stretched out and rested in
the snow, but the old man and the guide began to shout
and make a terrible din. We had to move on. Our bodies
were full of pain and agony, our heads lolled from side
to side as if made of lead, and yet we had to mount the
ponies and continue onwards and upwards. The only
relief was the path's increasing width, as we snaked
through a landscape of massive boulders. The white
turban approached my father.

'Give me a revolver. I will go first. Here the robbers
love to wait behind the stones. I will kill them . . .'
My father conferred with Boris in French, and they
deemed it necessary to hand over a pistol, but for
the whole duration of the journey my father sat bolt
upright with a loaded, unclipped Browning in his hand.

He did not take his eyes off the white turban for a moment, as the latter seemed more likely to shoot us than any imaginary robbers. We climbed higher. The landscape became increasingly wild and starkly beautiful. The snow lay hard on the ground, glistening like a myriad of diamonds. But who could possibly admire the scenery during these excruciating hours? My boots felt like ice-packs, and my poor mother's clothes had frozen solid.

We began to descend. The path narrowed and wound again along the side of a vertiginous chasm. Our nerves and bodies were so exhausted that we could no longer trust our reflexes at the edge of yet another Gehenna. The old one roped our horses together and led them by a halter, while we stumbled behind on foot. Happily, this path was not as devilishly long as the last one, and soon it widened into a soft, emerald-green plateau. In the middle of this unlooked-for lawn stood a tall red tulip, glowing self-consciously in the sun like a great drop of blood. All four of us threw ourselves on the ground and lay semi-conscious for half an hour. The white turban, standing over us, showered us with undecipherable abuse; he bellowed until there was foam around his mouth, but it did not impress us in the least.

Finally we dragged ourselves up, and moved on. It was midday, and the sun was like a cruel furnace. In my confused state of mind I tried to decide which would be most painful – being frozen to ice or cremated. Then, for the second time, we heard the merry sound of a spring. The sound seemed to fill my father with a sudden and invincible energy. He dismounted and demanded his revolver back from the driver. The latter seemed so surprised that he did not think to protest, especially as my father ordered him to hold his tongue. 'It is time we had a rest!' my father said, categorically.

We unpacked our food. Hardboiled eggs and bread tasted simply regal, and water from the spring was like divine nectar. My mother could hardly move but she sighed with happiness when I ran to and from the spring, bringing water in a broken eggshell – the only cup our provisional stores could muster! We made jokes about this primitive table service, but would not have done so if we had known what lay before us. Having finished our meal, we curled up and slept in the open, foolishly exposed to the sun. When we woke up, our faces had taken on the blue-tinted ruddiness to which alcoholics are prone. I crawled to the spring and dipped my whole head into the water. My previously wet boots now stuck to my legs like dried skins. I lay beside the spring thinking of our cool villa in Samarkand, the leafy garden with its brindled shade. I looked towards the interior of the mountain chain – snowy fields stretched into the distance. I looked downwards – pass after rocky pass, here and there a rocky plateau. At least we were descending.

Soon, the guide woke up and urged us on. I was the only one to mount my horse without assistance. The others were racked by pain, as if newly tortured.

'Is it far to the next village?' my father wondered.

'*Bir tasch*,' replied the guide (that is, seven Russian verst or nearly eight kilometres).

The track continued plunging downwards, and the heat became unbearable. It seemed to us that we were journeying into hell itself. After two hours, my father enquired again how many kilometres still lay before us. The answer was the same.

'*Bir tasch* . . .'

'Surely not, when we have travelled for another two hours?' he cried in exasperation. But our driver was not impressed.

'*Bir tasch*,' he said with great calm. It was our

61

sixteenth hour on horseback, and still our goal was out of sight. Another weary hour passed, sluggish and heavy.

It was my turn to ask, 'Will we be there soon?'

'*Bir tasch*,' came his confident reply.

The old man at the rear of the party rode up to the guide and started a conversation which deteriorated into a dispute. They interrupted each other, making furious gestures with their hands. We were too tired to attach any significance to this – it seemed the usual Sart way of conducting a discussion. Then our guide produced a long dagger from inside his tunic, and started waving it under the nose of the old man, while his eyes shone with murder and blood-lust. They dropped their reins, and such torrents of hatred seemed to flow out of them that one imagined they would both be damned for ever. Suddenly the old man took up his reins, swung about, and galloped back the way we had come. He was a tough old campaigner. Without food or rest he embarked on another sixteen-hour journey, and he must have been nearly seventy years old. I watched him torment his beast, whipping it on towards the snowy heights and paths of agony. Why he had come and why he left in this manner, we never found out. Under more normal conditions we would have responded to this mysterious event, but our brains could conceive of only one thought and one fervent desire: cool shade, cool shade, and sleep, sleep in the cool shade, sleep in the cool shade.

How we managed to survive the next few hours I will never know. After nineteen hours, none of us could manage another moment on horseback. Stumbling on our own feet, partly leading the ponies and partly resting against their strong flanks, we made slow progress over the stony ground. Through a haze of exhaustion, we saw two huts, a stable of cut stone, a mill, and a herd of sheep resting in the shade under a few trees. A fast-flowing river blessed this delightful pastoral scene; we crossed the span of a humble wooden bridge and went down to the torrent; immediately we sank down along its sandy bank and plunged our heads into its cool maelstrom, while the horses sucked the water alongside. Through a curtain of water I saw, on the opposite bank, a long canary-yellow snake lift its missile-shaped head, turn it towards me, and then make a hasty escape. Not even a dragon would have been able to drive me away from this fresh and blessed water. We were astonished to see an old man with a white beard standing smiling on his threshold. He nodded like the most benign pixie imaginable, and invited us to come inside. He asked if we desired to eat something, but we shook our heads, unable even to speak. We moved into the shade and peace of his dwelling and dropped down on the rugs, falling into an immediate swoon that resembled death.

9

Karamatilla!

After twelve hours of deep sleep, we stirred at around eight in the evening. Our limbs were so stiff that we could hardly move at all. My mother's legs were covered in ugly saddle sores, and her feet were swollen and bloody. Our situation seemed to demand prolonged rest, so that we could regain physical fitness.

The benevolent old man loomed up with a great dish of boiled chicken, rice, bread, and a pot of green tea. It tasted very fine. We could hear his wives talking in the hut next to ours, but were prevented from seeing them even though they were the ones who had prepared our food.

A group of tall, bearded riders thundered over the bridge and dismounted to water their horses. Their dark eyes shone with curiosity when they set eyes on us – shaven, light-skinned Europeans. They approached, curious as children, touching and pinching our clothes, giggling in wonderment at the sight of such odd people. Their delight became downright jubilation when they discovered my mother's pocket mirror; sporadic bouts of fighting broke out as they strove to reflect their wild faces in this enchanted glass. For hours they sat like grimacing apes, examining themselves from every conceivable angle, frequently breaking into roars of hilarity. Finally, and with much regret, they parted with the magical object, and set off. Their destination was the same as ours – the town of Kitab – and we realised that soon the whole population would know that we were approaching. During our travels in Turkistan, we often remarked that our comings held no surprise. News in the East spreads from mouth to mouth with the speed of forked lightning, much like a telephone service without the encumbrance of electrical cables.

The following morning the white turban rode to Kitab to make an official announcement to the Bej that a small group of Russians were coming to his town. We waited a whole day for his return, but finally despaired of him, and set off in the afternoon with our pleasant host as guide. Compared with previous misadventures, this was a relatively painless day's travelling. In addition, we were hugely entertained by a band of Sart riders who attached themselves to our party. They could not get enough of my mother, whose face was unveiled and palely European. This fired their passions. In addition, her ample girth appealed to their sense of beauty, and they were constantly crying out with worshipful and devoted appeals. My father and Boris were subjected to a barrage of insatiable questions, none of which they could understand. And the Sart riders laughed so that they almost tumbled off their horses when I greeted a nearby pair of storks in the native Turki language. '*Salamalejkum, lajlak-djon!* – Good day to you Mr Stork . . .' To entice them into another wild expression of joy, I cried out to a passing camel, '*Salamalejkum, tuja-djon!* – Good day to you, Mr Camel . . .' But their roars of approbation were such that I did not dare continue in the same vein.

Towards evening, Kitab rose up before us. Like all towns in Bokhara it was encircled by high walls. At ten o'clock the town's gates swung open for us. Evidently we were expected. A sentry announced to us in Russian that we would shortly be taken to the Bej. Matters of etiquette were also detailed – how our hands should be held, and bows performed.

The Bej received us with some graciousness, and listened to my father's assurances that far from being Bolsheviks, we were in flight from their repression. He seemed convinced. A sumptuous meal was set before us. His two sons served us pilau, bread, raisins and candied fruits, as well as soured milk and tea. At this same moment, as we later found out, the white turban was languishing in a medieval torture chamber, arrested as a likely Bolshevik spy. His head, hands and feet were locked into stocks. Certainly we were not overly fond of the white turban, but our appetites would have been dulled if we had known of his fate.

The night was spent on the earth floor of a *chai-khana* (teahouse). In the morning, a handsome man from the Bej's personal guard presented himself to us and offered to lead us to the next town of Schaar-Schaus, across the green reaches of the steppe which at this time of the year was still full of blooming flowers. Soon after setting off, we came to a wide river, only a metre or so deep. As we carefully urged our horses into the water, we heard a ringing voice from the opposite bank: 'Well, hello,' came the pleasant cry. And there, his horse rearing up picturesquely, was a rider who seemed to have ridden straight out of a fairytale, a further visitation from *A Thousand and One Nights*. He was tall, slender, imposing. His fiery eyes shone like embers, and his white teeth flashed through an ample beard and moustache. On his head he wore a white turban, and beneath his sky-blue kaftan a belt of gold and gemstones. The horse danced exquisitely and frothed over its silver bridle studded with big turquoise stones.

It was this radiant presence which was calling to us, and which added, in faultless Russian, 'Do my eyes deceive me, or is it the bank director I see . . . ?'

The voice was familiar, and my father eventually responded, with astonishment.

'Can it really be you, Karamatilla? What are you doing here . . . and in those clothes?'

Karamatilla threw back his head and laughed; satisfied with the effect he had produced, and spurring his horse, which took one great leap into the river, he rode up to my mother and, like a true chevalier, kissed her hand. 'Is there something wrong with my clothes? They are the clothes of my land . . . or would you have me dress as a European?' He continued, more to the point: 'I know you are going to Schaar-Schaus. I have come from there with a message for Kitab, but I shall soon be back again . . .' In a commanding voice, Karamatilla cried some words in Turki to our Sart guide, who bowed reverentially. Then once more he spurred his horse. '*Dosvidanie!*' he cried. 'Farewell . . . we shall meet again . . .'

With this, he galloped off through the water so that it sparkled all around him like a bright halo, competing with his array of jewels. His exit was as effective – and as theatrical – as his entrance. For the rest of the journey we could talk of nothing but this man. In Samarkand it had always been assumed that he was immeasurably wealthy; this in spite of the fact that he lived off the proceeds of his cinema, the only one in Samarkand, which he had named 'Progress Pictures'. Karamatilla had always been one of the town's most flamboyant and pivotal figures. Although Asiatic, he had only ever shown himself in European clothes; hence our amazement when we beheld him on the steppe.

On the other hand, Karamatilla had always been extravagant when it came to his wardrobe. A client at my father's bank, many times he had had to endure irksome suggestions to cut his expenditure on clothes. One particular morning, Karamatilla had made an

67

appearance at the bank dressed in black tie and dinner-jacket, with big diamond cufflinks; delightedly, he had turned up his trousers to display the sumptuous silk lining. The stern advice that such clothes should not be worn before noon was received with deep disdain.

His personable charm made one wish to overlook his faults. Karamatilla's parties were famous in Samarkand, and invitations were much sought after, even though many Russians would not go to the house of an Asian. The hostess at these gatherings was a radiant beauty from Moscow, a tall, lithe woman who at breakfast time would already be in full dress, wearing diamonds. Her alluring blue eyes, brimming with sensuous longing, would follow every movement of her handsome young lover. A more glamorous and harmonious couple one could not wish to see. Her beauty was heightened by the contrast with this Aladdin, whose Eastern eyes glittered proudly when he beheld his European lady. A year before our departure, Karamatilla had suddenly disappeared from Samarkand.

Our minds were so preoccupied with him, that before we knew it, a tall red tower appeared on the horizon. We had arrived at Schaar-Schaus. As we drew closer, we discovered a group of soldiers in peculiar uniforms, squatting in front of the town gates by great piles of vegetables, which they were trying to sell. At the sight of us they jumped to their feet, hurriedly put on their hats, picked up their rifles, and performed some perfunctory salutes. The gates were wide open. They were obviously anxious to present themselves with as much pomp as could be mustered. They were wearing the regimental headwear of the old Imperial Army; on to their Sart kaftans they had stitched epaulettes of varying colours and origins – some even wore different decorations on each shoulder. Along the front of the kaftans various gaudy buttons, military in origin, had been attached.

We tried to look suitably impressed, greeted them with a 'salamalejkum', and rode through the gate of Schaar–Schaus. Our guide showed us to the *chai-khana* where we would lodge. He had been unusually civil, and my father wanted to give him something as a measure of our gratitude. Finding a silver cup in his saddle bag – actually, a fairly indifferent object – he handed it to the man, who became transported with delight at this princely gift. Struck dumb, his gaze flickered in disbelief, gazing at the beloved object and then at my father. Suddenly he threw himself into the saddle and galloped out through the city gates. Maybe he was worried that we would change our minds; whatever the case, his gratitude was altogether disproportionate.

10

In the Hands of the Bej

Our most pressing duty now was to arrange for an audience with the Bej, but as he only spoke Turki we decided to wait for Karamatilla: he would be the very best of interpreters. We had hoped to see him within a few hours, as he had intimated at our meeting; but evening came, and there was no sign of him. Resignedly we sat on the trunks, looking out through the doors of the *chai-khana*. Across a square, high stone walls encircled the Bej's residence. Beyond the ramparts was a minaret some forty metres high, with a pair of graceful storks nesting on top. Having nothing else to do, we watched these birds descend repeatedly to the irrigation ditches in the streets, where they deftly speared frogs and carried them on their last journey, to the heavens.

After several hours I plucked up courage to go into the hubbub of the bazaar and search for fresh fruit. But my small presence provoked such overbearing fascination that I thought it best to retire to the *chai-khana*; I arrived with an escort of street-boys, whose amusement had done some damage to my manly pride. We waited until nightfall for our interpreter; finally we gave up and fell asleep on the floor, our heads propped up awkwardly against our luggage.

Night was shorter than we had anticipated. At five in the morning, we were awakened by a tremendous commotion. I stuck my head out of the door and saw a motley band of musicians in full swing beneath the Bej's great walls. Some of them regaled us with small flutes, while a soloist blew on a clarinet large as a bassoon and so heavy that a retainer had to support it on his shoulder. The percussion section was rudimentary – one man beat a bass drum, divine fury evident in his whole being, while another extracted rhythm from an upturned tin bath. Beside the musicians stood a troop of twenty soldiers, whose uniforms were as fantastical as those of the sentries at the gate. The commander outshone them all by wearing three epaulettes on each shoulder. The soldiers seemed to be suffering from some terrible affliction, for they were constantly itching every possible area of their bodies. The sight of these scratching warriors accompanied by the raving music was too much for me. I broke into peals of laughter, which was probably ill-advised, for my father drew me inside and closed the door.

We soon realised that our stay in Schaar-Schaus would be prolonged. Every morning we were woken up by the same infernal cacophony. We reached the conclusion that the band of men were the Bej's personal guard – and the orchestral sounds the reveille of Schaar-Schaus! A governor who liked to start the day in this manner must in truth be viewed as an uncommon lover of music!

Later in the day we would venture into the bazaar, which was a modest version of the one in Samarkand. We particularly admired a pair of Orientals who strolled about with lordly nonchalance in *khalats* of gold brocade and lustrous sash belts. The spice fairs provided an effective backdrop. Here, dark Indians sat in their niches like immobile Buddhas, red cast-marks daubed on their foreheads.

One afternoon, to our relief, Karamatilla arrived, and the time of our audience with the Bej was arranged. My mother was forbidden to accompany us, as it was beneath the dignity of the Bej to be confronted by a woman not wearing a veil. The great man's dwelling was surprisingly austere. He was sitting cross-legged on a large cushion on the floor. His turban was of white silk and his kaftan of damask but his trousers were blatantly filthy, tucked into embroidered red Moroccan boots. The long white beard, which reached down to the floor, seemed to be attached to his hooked nose. As previously instructed, we put our hands against our chests and stooped low; he gestured to us, and we sat down at a precise distance of two metres from his throne.

Karamatilla spoke on our behalf, as this Bej did not know a single word of Russian. We listened breathlessly, and then Karamatilla bowed again, and turned to us. Speaking with deep gravity, he said, 'The old idiot thought you were Bolsheviks, but I have put his fears to rest. Now you have to give him your weapons or the ass will think you're going to shoot him . . .'

Boris and my father edged forward and reverently placed their pistols before the Bej, who swivelled his hooked nose and spoke a few brief words into Karamatilla's ear. The latter, after a brief pause, translated, 'His Grace the Bej of Schaar-Schaus informs you that permission to continue to Bokhara must be witheld until such a time that the Emir of Bokhara has given his personal consent. The Bej will therefore send a courier to his Graciousness the Emir of Bokhara, with a view to procuring such a document . . .'

'Tell him,' my father intervened, 'that I am a personal friend of the Emir of Bokhara, that I have manufactured a machine for his mint, and in appreciation of this I have been decorated with the Order of the Brilliant Star . . .'

Karamatilla translated this, and listened to the muttered reply. 'This lofty fool,' he told us, 'does not believe

72

you, and he takes you for a liar. He will not let you go until he has the permit from Bokhara. He's as frightened of the Emir as a hare. But don't worry,' Karamatilla said, 'I shall make certain that you live comfortably while waiting here. And this old bloodsucker will pay for it . . . one thing he does not lack is money, and that is the truth!'

Once again, Karamatilla turned to the Bej, murmured a few courteous phrases, and bowed. The audience was over. As we walked away, Karamatilla clenched his teeth and said, 'To swines like that I have to abase myself! I have no choice in the matter. When I come to you tonight I shall tell you why . . .'

11

The Tales of Karamatilla

That evening I got my first real opportunity to gauge the measure of Karamatilla's charisma, and his piquant mixture of the European and Oriental. He had faultless manners and an uncanny gift for humour and sympathetic insight. This sense of intuition meant that he was adept at getting people to forget their troubles. The general atmosphere was morose, but after an hour in the company of Karamatilla, we felt that life – in spite of everything – was full of promise.

'Just wait,' he said. 'Before you know it the courier will be here with a permit from the Emir. And then let's buy a wagon with soft suspension and upholstered seats – and a good thatched roof. I'll locate a trustworthy guide, and within a few days we'll be in Bokhara . . .'

'Are you coming with us, then?' my father asked.

'Of course,' said Karamatilla. 'Surely you don't think I'll be spending the rest of my life here. You couldn't even imagine what a hellish time I've had in this execrable dump. For eight months now I've worked for this Bej, as secretary and interpreter . . . in other words, ever since they nationalised my cinema and house in Kaufmann Street. When they began to sniff at Vera's diamonds, we'd finally had enough.' He paused. 'Like you, we thought it best to escape . . .'

'So she is here as well?' my mother enquired.

'No, the Bej would have beheaded me at once if I

had dared show myself in Schaar-Schaus with a Russian woman. Happily, Vera was able to get to Persia before it was too late. She is in Teheran at present, and I believe she is well. If I get as far as Bokhara then I hope you won't object to my company beyond there . . .'

'It would be a pleasure,' said my father. 'But with your declared allegiance to the Emir you surely have no need to share our visa? Aren't you free to go as you please?'

'No, far from it! This land is more plagued with officialdom than China. Everyone is under suspicion, on some trumped-up charge. I also came here by way of Kitab, and there they wanted to imprison me because I dared show myself without a beard . . . in breach of Koranic law!'

'Was the Bej suspicious of you too? Did he fear that you were a Bolshevik?'

'Oh yes, you can be sure of that! But I knew how to deal with an avaricious old magpie like him. I put on my most valuable belt.' He pointed at his precious girdle. 'And I wore my largest diamond rings. The Bej couldn't take his eyes off them as soon as I walked into his chambers. When I took off the most valuable ring and gave it to him, our friendship was sealed. He snatches whatever he wants – everything from jewels to young girls. No one dares go against him, his power is limitless. In Schaar-Schaus his power is greater than Mohammed himself. You see, no Bej of the Emir's is paid more than two roubles a year for his duties. As a result each levies punitive taxes during his term of office . . . but this Bej is worse than anyone else. He is the only judge and practitioner of the law in these parts, and his punishments are exceptionally severe, apart from those occasions when a bribe is large enough to merit an acquittal. Lately he has been gloating over my belt, so I suppose I'll have to part from it soon . . .'

I asked to see the magnificent object, and he immediately took it off. Together we admired the exquisite workmanship. I let my fingers glide over the golden smoky topaz. These were large as hens' eggs, and surrounded by clusters of amethysts, sapphires and pearls. The plates of gold were attached to a red-tanned belt of Moroccan leather. On its inside there was a small pocket secured with a cabochon sapphire clip. I fingered this gorgeous light-blue stone; but Karamatilla took the belt back, opened the pocket, and brought out a small piece of folded paper.

'This little note has a story,' he said, and seemed to falter for an instant. 'Because you are my friends I'm going to tell it to you. I don't want to keep you in the dark. In actual fact I did not flee Samarkand because my property was nationalised, as I said this morning. The true reason is that the Bolsheviks discovered that I was spying for the Emir of Bokhara. How they managed to find that out I'll never know. Perhaps you think it strange that I didn't divulge this information earlier, but I have learnt to practice restraint. One cannot be careful enough in these times. People should not be trusted until one has tested them. And I have done this now.

'As soon as the Bolsheviks had caught me, they flung me into gaol. If it had happened today I would have been shot without trial, but eight months ago there was more lenience in Samarkand. Vera and I had begun planning our escape to Persia when this misfortune befell us. She postsponed her own escape and waited for news of me.

'In the prison they were decent enough to let me smoke a *kaljan* – a Sart waterpipe – and this proved to be my blessing. After many fruitless attempts, Vera was finally allowed to visit me in my cell. At an opportune moment she whispered to me that all the preparations for our escape had been made.

'After she had left, I took my *kaljan* and smoked all day. In the night I drank the water at the bottom of the pipe. Of course, it was heavily dosed with nicotine. Things went exactly as I planned. I became violently ill, and started to vomit. And, of course, I pretended to be at death's door . . . Soon they carried me over to the hospital, as there was no sick bay in the prison. A sentry was put by my bed, but he seemed rather bored . . . from time to time he stretched his legs or took a glass of wine.

'After a while I began to stir from my "unconsciousness", and presently I asked the guard to go and buy me a bottle of vodka. This was a medicine in whose restorative powers he had much faith. It would surely give me new strength. We took turns to swig at the bottle, and little by little the guard realised that his life was not as mediocre as he had previously thought. Before too long he had decided that I could do with another bottle of medicine, and he promptly swanned off for this very purpose. By midnight, he was drunk as a pig. As I closed the door to my ward, he lay snoaring in my bed. He must have had an unpleasant awakening!

'I ran to a nearby house where Vera was awaiting me with a horse and a Turki shepherd's gown. When dawn broke I was already high in the Hissar Mountains. At the very same time, an immaculately veiled woman boarded a train at the station outside Samarkand. Close to her body, gathered up in a girdle, she carried a valuable cache of diamonds. With this treasure trove she set off for Bokhara, where we had arranged a rendezvous. But this was not to be. I was detained, and it proved impossible for me to reach the Emir's city. Hence she journeyed on to Teheran. I stayed on here as the Bej's secretary. But now I have high hopes that I shall reach Bokhara in your company . . . And so I come to the

77

story of this scrap of paper.' He balanced it in the palm of his hand.

'A few months ago a Russian arrived here, by name of Ivanov. He was brought before the Bej, who interrogated him with my help. We couldn't get to grips with the man, weren't sure if he were fish or fowl, but I promised the Bej that I would get to the bottom of it . . . Ivanov was staying in this very teahouse, and that night we sat drinking tea together, just as we are doing now. Ivanov told me that he had fled from the Bolsheviks, and that he intended to go to Bokhara and from there join up with General Malleson's army. He hoped to get a commission . . . I was also sleeping in the teahouse. When we had retired to bed and put out the lights, I took Ivanov by the arm, and said to him, "My friend, you don't have to fear me. You surely can't believe that I am here of my own free will, in this damned Schaar-Schaus? I've been despatched here by the komissars in Samarkand to get information on Bokhara's plotting against the Soviet."

'I knew all the komissars in Samarkand, and it was easy to gain his confidence with a few details. Soon I had duped him and instilled a dangerous sense of security. He opened his heart and told me that he was also a spy for the Soviet. He asked me to help him get to Bokhara so that he could fulfil his assignment, which was to get precise logistical information on the Emir's resources: weapons, soldiers, troop concentrations, defensive strategies. The Bolsheviks, as everyone knew, were planning an imminent attack on Bokhara.

'I promised to help him, and he fell into an untroubled sleep. I also slept well, for I knew that I had uncovered a traitor. In the morning I reported my findings to the Bej, and he asked me to take care of the matter as discreetly as possible. And so we saddled our horses and set off for Bokhara – or so Ivanov thought. Before we left, I told

78

him that soon I would be returning to Samarkand to be debriefed by the commission. If he wished, I would take back a message for his wife and mother, whom he'd talked of at length. He had told me that they were deeply worried about the outcome of his perilous expedition. He thanked me delightedly, and wrote this message . . .' Karamatilla handed us the paper. It went from hand to hand, and I read, 'Dearest Mother and Ljuba. I have found a friend who is helping me. I am in good heart and health. Today I am setting off for Bokhara. With my love, Ivanov.'

Karamatilla took the note back, and with a distracted smile he tucked it back into the pocket of his belt. 'I asked him to write this, so that if there were any unwelcome investigations, the Bej would have some solid evidence . . .'

'Well, what happened to Ivanov?' Boris asked.

'Oh yes, we rode out of Schaar-Schaus. It was a stifling hot day, and a few miles out on the hot steppe I suggested that we should stop and refresh ourselves with some tea. We collected some twigs and put the kettle in the fire. I picked up my rifle and stood behind him. He turned around and asked me what I was doing. I told him that I thought I had seen a jackal . . . I sat down next to him and we drank our tea. Again I got up with my rifle, while Ivanov was fixing himself a second cup of tea. Just as he was bringing the cup to his mouth, I shot him from behind, through the neck. He dropped the cup, the tea hissed in the flames and Ivanov himself toppled into the fire. He didn't make a sound. I buried him in the sand. I shall show his letter to the Emir of Bokhara. It will be a letter of recommendation for me.'

He laughed melodiously, and watched our dismayed faces with a certain satisfaction. 'Don't look at me like that!' he said. 'That's exactly how a Bolshevik dog

79

should die . . .' Again he smiled his winning smile, and his eyes glowed with benevolence and friendship. But we felt cold inside, sitting there on the mud floor of the dingy little *chai-khana*. The atmosphere became oppressive. It was intolerable to us that such a charming and exquisite being could be so cruel and devoid of feeling. We drew a sigh of relief when the charming murderer left.

'We have to be on our guard with Karamatilla,' said my father. 'Do not criticise him, or gainsay him. Do not even laugh when he ridicules the Bej. Karamatilla is capable of anything. He's as dangerous as he is beautiful . . .'

12

Aladdin's Fate

Karamatilla came to us every morning, ever well-groomed and full of impeccable intentions. He played chess and cards with us, and kept us entertained with numerous tales. This was an attempt to ward off our inevitable boredom, for day after day passed without word from Bokhara.

Occasionally, a pair of devout Sarts squatted outside our hovel and mumbled their interminable prayers. To our tired ears they sounded anything but sacred. And the barbaric orchestra roused us punctually at five every morning. One night, however, our rest was disturbed at four o'clock by hideous screams. It was impossible to mistake the piteous calls of someone in mortal agony. At long last the screams became more subdued, and anxiously we listened as they subsided into a low whimpering. When Karamatilla arrived, he put our nervous curiosity to rest.

The Bej, it appeared, had taken it upon himself to punish a thief. The unfortunate man was held down while his illustrious judge and ruler beat him to death with a stick. This was his punishment for stealing a melon in the bazaar. Such executions were popular public spectacles, attracting enthusiastic crowds. No one was more zealous than the Bej when it came to punishing transgressions; he even fought bouts with a high civil servant of the town, in the presence of an

81

umpire, to establish who would have the honour of administering the chastisement.

The Sarts loved to see flowing blood. One day we chanced upon two men who had drawn long knives and were eagerly stabbing and slashing at each other. No one tried to intervene – far from it. Instead, people sat down around them, and urged them on with encouraging cries. Only when the men sank to the ground, exhausted and bleeding from deep wounds, did the audience scatter. People walked away grateful for this unexpected pleasure. Blood and gold were the only things that could arouse them from their characteristic apathy.

Every day the Bej sallied forth on his white horse decked with silver adornments. Bowing and fawning Sarts surrounded him as he rode out to 'inspect' his town. The bazaar was the special focus of his stern interest. He personally weighed the bread at the bakeries to establish that no one was being cheated of a full measure of flour. Any irregularity was punishable with twenty-five lashes, and this was considered lenient. After such an ordeal, the 'criminal' would be bedridden for months. But if a law-breaker were served with fifty lashes, he had to submit to his chastisement in instalments. First he was given twenty-five lashes and then, having spent some months recuperating, he was given the remaining twenty-five. The physical sentence was followed by the moral censure of the community. The criminal was required to wander in the lanes of the bazaar, calling out his name, his crime and his punishment. And then he had to add: 'I have received my due, and I thank the Lord and the high Bej for judging me . . .' The law extended to every area of life. There were punishments for shaving, for cutting one's beard, for showing disrespect to one's superiors. Fear ruled in

Schaar-Schaus, and the Bej was the personification of cruelty itself.

Prudently we kept in the background as much as possible, and finally, after a week, were rewarded by the return of the courier with our exit visas. We immediately sold two of our horses. Boris and I would ride the remaining two, while my parents were to travel in a cart bought for that purpose. On our departure, the Bej informed us that our revolvers would be returned in Bokhara.

In early May we drove out through the city gates; the burlesque guards, once more, abandoned their stalls of vegetables and saluted us. After half an hour, we were out on a steppe already burnt to cinders by the relentless sun. The driver was mounted on the horse pulling the *arba* – and Boris, Karamatilla and I rode behind in a troop. Suddenly Karamatilla pointed to a little mound by the side of the path. He did not need to tell us that this was Ivanov's grave. When he saw our darkening faces, he defended himself.

'A death like this is the easiest of all. If the fool had made it to Bokhara he would have been tortured to death. Haven't you heard for yourselves what it sounds like when a mere thief is punished in this land?'

'Are there no humane executions?' I asked.

'Oh yes, young man. Have you ever observed how we slaughter our sheep? One man holds the front legs and another pins the hind legs down. A third man puts his knee across the animal's breast and holds it fast. Then he takes a long knife and slits the throat . . . the blood runs into a depression in the ground . . .' Karamatilla stopped and analysed my reaction. 'That is how they execute people in these parts. In the past, they used to throw them down from the Tower of Death, but the Imperial Government made that illegal. Now people are simply slaughtered like dumb beasts. If I could choose

83

between the stick and the knife I think I would have the latter.' He smiled at me, light-heartedly. 'Or what would you prefer?'

We continued moving all day, without a single rest. After sundown a blood-red moon rose, and the wind started gusting over the steppe. Clouds of sand were whipped up, filling the sky. The moon changed colour, became lime yellow. The steppe was flat as a sheet of steel, and the wind howled all around us, expertly ferrying handfuls of sand into our clothes, eyes and throats. It became a painful journey. I remember the wind and the yellow moon. Our driver, who seemed impervious to the weather, sat on his horse singing melancholy songs. At midnight we crossed the railway line connecting Samarkand with Bokhara. After a further half-hour, Karamatilla said, 'Now we are out of danger. Here we could have chanced upon a Bolshevik patrol, and then we would have been doomed. Tomorrow afternoon we'll be in Bokhara . . .'

At three in the morning, half-blinded and exhausted, we stumbled into a caravanserai, and set up camp amongst horses and camels. A flickering paraffin lamp lit up a section of the wall, and before I fell asleep I saw the lice crawling over the wickerwork. In disgust I turned away. Through the branches and leaves of the ceiling, two yellow snakes came slithering with great stealth. I fell asleep.

At first light we set forth again, and after another long day, the ramparts of Bokhara appeared on the horizon. By seven in the evening we stood before the gates of the city but they had already been closed; however, Bokhara had long outgrown its straitjacket, and extended far beyond the old walls. We found a caravanserai without difficulty. We even managed to secure a room this time, with an actual window! From the rafters hung a row of cages with quails, piping their monotonous little ditties.

We sat down in the doorway and lost ourselves in the romantic spectacle unfolding before us; if this were not the East, then no such place existed in the world! Meandering caravans approached and halted before the high walls; irate camels gurgled and brawled, and, as a measure of their disrespect, spat gobs of saliva at their unconcerned drivers.

On top of a trench, a rusty, antiquated cannon had been positioned; below, the half-hearted soldiers of a detachment were going through their drill. They were in a sorry state. If this was a fair sample of the Emir's army, then his fate was sealed even before the Bolsheviks attacked. We did not see a single Russian, nor a European building of any description. And always, beyond and above every roof, the great ochre walls reared up, with the imposing *pishtaq* – Arabic portal. Beyond the walls was a tower incomparably higher than any other edifice. Egyptian doves wheeled around its sun-touched apex; the intricate mosaics glowed in the ruby-coloured light. We stood in mute admiration.

'That is the Tower of Death,' said Karamatilla. 'Kalyar Minar . . .' he continued dreamily. 'From its upper windows the Emir used to fling off his prisoners . . . that is, until the Czar outlawed the practice. Perhaps the Tower will have a new lease of life now that Bokhara has announced its independence.' From a minaret a mullah called out the *shahada*. Sarts fell on their knees all about us, and began to mumble their prayers. Karamatilla was filled with loathing.

'Such superstition . . .'

'But it's a fine sight, wouldn't you say, to see the honour in which they hold their Lord?' my father responded. Karamatilla shrugged his shoulders.

Suddenly, two elderly and well-dressed Sarts stood before us. Because our attention had been elsewhere, it was as if they had risen up from the earth. They

85

did not pay the slightest heed to us. Instead they addressed Karamatilla, who got to his feet. For a moment I thought that his bronze skin went pale, but it must have been a trick of the light; with his usual jocular manner he waved to us all: 'I'll see you tomorrow,' he said. 'In town . . .' And with this, he was escorted away by the two men. For a while, we were puzzled. We tried to guess where he had gone, and on what business. But our spirits were high after concluding the first stage of our long journey. We put on the kettle and made some green tea, and then sat back on the mud floor and built elaborate castles in the clouds. We talked about all the comfortable chairs and sofas we would purchase in Vienna. A villa would be rented, and a car with a chauffeur. 'And you're getting a whole new set of clothes, and a black tie and dinner jacket,' my father laughed as he playfully dragged me across the floor by my filthy kaftan. It was easy to lose ourselves in fantasy: in our saddlebags we carried two million roubles in banknotes, and the Bank Verein in Vienna had received and deposited a sum of 750,000 Austrian crowns. Even allowing for the plummeting exchange rate of the rouble, these were ample sums of money.

The riviera had to be visited, and Paris, and Denmark – where my father came from.

'And you'll have to see Sweden, where your Swedish princess lives,' my father joked.

'What princess?' Boris quizzed. 'I've never heard anything about a Swedish princess . . .'

'Oh that . . . that was one of my greatest adventures,' I told him. 'And it happened while you were still based in St Petersburg . . .'

'Well, let's hear it then!'

But the sun had gone down, and the sultry night was upon us. We were exhausted after our travails, and my story was a long one. I promised Boris that I would entertain him with some details during our forthcoming desert journey, and he seemed satisfied with that.

In the morning, the two mysterious Sarts were once again at our door, asking this time for Karamatilla's bags. My father pointed to his saddle-bags on the floor. They examined the contents with careful deliberation. When they discovered the girdle, they opened the inside pocket and brought out Ivanov's letter, which they tried, in vain, to read. In the end they discarded it on the floor, and disappeared with all of Karamatilla's belongings.

I picked up Ivanov's note and decided to keep it hidden. Later on, a mullah stuck his head through our door and asked if we were the people who had been travelling with Karamatilla. We overwhelmed him with our questions, demanding to know where our friend had been taken. The mullah, by way of a reply, pulled a finger across his throat.

'But why?' we cried. 'Why?'

'Karamatilla spy for the Bolsheviks, Karamatilla spy also for the Emir,' whispered the mullah. He had witnessed the execution. It had been carried out in exactly the way that Karamatilla, with a wry smile on his lips, had once recommended.

I saved Ivanov's letter for many years, but every time I looked at it there was a burning pain in my heart as the memories came flooding back. Eventually I relegated it to the fire. It was my only keepsake of that Aladdin who had ridden straight out of the jaws of a cruel fairytale and with his smiling black eyes and white teeth, worshipped by women, admired by men, good as a child, cruel as a tiger, had been slaughtered by a sharp knife to the throat, as when the Sarts kill their sheep and let the blood run into a depression in the ground.

13

The First Caravan

In spite of our valid entry visas, the gates remained closed to us for another three days.

Our identity papers were scrutinised with extreme caution by the city's chief governor, Kush-Begi. As soon as this powerful man realised that it was my father who had manufactured the machinery for Bokhara's mint, all further obstacles were removed. We were invited to settle permanently in the city, where, it was suggested, my father should establish some factories. He was flattered by this proposal, but life was dearer to us than any transient honours – and we were convinced that every delay would sit heavy on the scales of our doom. The Red Army was getting closer every day. Bokhara's fall was imminent – and our fears were strengthened by swift rumours in free circulation amongst the Russian community of the city. This colony comprised some thirty individuals, refugees from revolutionary committees in Samarkand and Kagan; before long, they were part of our daily lives. Many delays could be expected before the next leg of our journey, so a small two-roomed apartment was rented in the bazaar, next to the mosque. One of the mullahs from the mosque made a noisy protest that the purity of Mohammed's shrine should not be defiled by dirty and faithless European dogs. He calmed himself, however, once he realised that the dirty dogs did not indulge in any form of propaganda on behalf of their unholy gods.

Our house became the meeting place for friends and campaigners, united in exile. Stories abounded of unlikely destinies and, of course, many a miraculous escape! Through all the accounts, like a long red thread, ran the dread of the Bolsheviks' growing power.

Even Bondy found his way to us – he of my last, ill-fated birthday party. Somehow he had managed to slip through the cordon of guards and patrols around Samarkand, and now he implored my father to allow him passage with the caravan that was in full preparation. His nails were varnished and his palms dyed, and when we noticed all this elegance pertaining to Sart femininity, he laughed and explained that he had disguised himself thus, and covered his face with a veil. It had been an easy matter, especially as he knew a number of phrases in Turki, and was famously adept at speaking in a falsetto voice. But his hands and nails had been dyed with such strong pigments that, notwithstanding his attempts to wash off the tell-tale marks, he remained highly decorative.

Bondy's fiancée had stayed behind in Samarkand. She had evaded jail by putting her stenographic skills at the disposal of the committee, where she now worked until such time that she could get out.

Bondy also related to us the sensation caused by our escape. It was said that we had got away with two million roubles in gold, and jewellery worth as much again. The villa had been turned over, and then nationalised as the future Bolshevik Academy. Twenty-eight people had moved in without delay, one family in each room, and after a prolonged civil war the furniture and contents of the house had been shared out among the new occupants. Some 'friends' of ours had

89

annexed all the carpets. The garden had been swiftly turned into a pig farm.

Many compatriots wanted to join our caravan, while others dissuaded us from ever attempting to leave Bokhara. The desert, they argued, was synonymous with death. Others advised us to head north towards the Aral Sea, where General Denikin's White Army was based, or to take the southern road to Merw where General Malleson kept his White troops.

When a Polish lady of our acquaintance heard of this latter possibility, she rushed over to our house and in floods of tears made us swear that we would not attempt this route. A German doctor with his wife and five children had recently done so, only to be captured by a band of Chiwini robbers. According to this Polish lady, the captives had been made to stand in a single file, and had then been felled by a single bullet. Undoubtedly a rare feat of markmanship! Their skeletons were discovered in the desert, having been picked clean by jackals. I have to admit that my imagination was stirred by such stories – I seemed to see my own bones glowing ghostly white in the desert sand.

My father was less affected by this terrified woman, who concluded her jeremiad with weeping because she did not have the courage to throw in her destiny with ours – even though she had a beautiful daughter of nineteen whose fate in the hands of the Reds was easy to predict.

After due consideration, my father chose the south-bound route through the Kara-Kul wastelands. Our goal would be the city of Merw. The driver we engaged, strikingly Christ-like in his appearance, claimed the journey would take no more than eight or nine days. Hudaj-Verdy, as he was named, carried himself with the grace of an unearthly king. When he passed by in his white robes, mounted on a donkey, the Russians often touched their temples in wonderment. Had they not seen the Master himself, from Nazareth? Pious members of the caravan took this as a good omen and saw Hudaj-Verdy as a guarantor of success in our undertaking.

My father had an immense amount of organising to do, and was given valuable assistance by another Samarkand refugee and an old customer at the bank. His name was Kalantarow. Still immeasurably rich in spite of constant losses suffered during the reign of the Bolsheviks, Kalantarow owned great tracts of land and almost infinite numbers of sheep. He was a member of the despised Jewish community of Bokhara, and was forced to comply with several official directives. In spite of his wealth, he was only to wear a simple woollen black kaftan – silk was strictly forbidden. While the Sarts outdid each other with golden belts, the Jews could only have a rough piece of rope around their stomachs. Whosoever wished to strike or kick a Jew could do so with impunity, whether the latter were a beggar or a millionaire. Nor could a Jew even have the pleasure of riding a horse; only the humble donkey was deemed suitable for him. Kalantarow told us about these regulations, not without a certain humorous acceptance, as if the suffering of his race were a necessity, a fact of nature. When he saw our sympathetic faces, he tried to enlighten us to his true plight – he turned up the hem of his trousers and showed us what a stylish man he was after all! The lining was of silk. He also allowed us a quick peek at the large diamonds which, albeit furtively, were worn on the insides of his shirtsleeves. Of what importance was the hatred of Sarts when one could walk encased in silk and diamonds?

With the help of Kalantarow, the preparations advanced quickly. To protect our caravan from robbers we would attach ourselves to a large Jewish merchants' caravan transporting astrakhan furs to Merw. This latter caravan was setting off very soon, and so we had very little notice: the next few days were fraught with last-minute, frantic attempts at securing food supplies and extra pack animals. Our driver, Hudaj-Verdy, assured us that it was unnecessary to buy new waterskins, for after no more than a night's ride we would arrive at the oasis of Kara-Kul, where his house was; and there, he promised, we could take over his own waterskins for half the price of new ones. This idea, which seemed reasonable at the time, was later the cause of much misery. One last task remained: to find and purchase *hidjevas*, which can only be translated as 'riding boxes'. Each camel carries two such boxes, one on either side of the hump, and in them two passengers recline while the desert ship makes its stately progress. Thick wadded quilts and cushions are used to soften the unkind edges of the wooden *hidjeva*.

The day before our departure, two diminutive men, half-starved and caked in thick dirt, found their way to us. They were Czech prisoners of war, both of them officers. Bina and Tamhina pleaded with us to make room for them in our caravan, and as they had already hired their own camel we could reply in the affirmative without detriment to our cause. And on the morning of the ultimate day, there was yet another fugitive, from Taschkent. He was a lawyer who went by the same name as Lenin – Uljanow. A little too sure of himself, his haughty manner woke antipathy in us all. But he was a countryman and, after all, we were all fleeing the same foe: death.

The authorities harassed us with every conceivable formality. For the second time the customs men rifled through our supplies and wanted to confiscate our silver cutlery, on the pretext that it was not suitable for desert life. Did we not know that in the desert one only had need of spoons? But a small and timely bribe caused them to change their views on the subject.

On 15 May our twenty-three camels stood, fully loaded, outside the gates of the city. We were to start first, followed by the fifty pack-animals of the Jewish caravan. Gathered around us were the Russians who had lacked courage to leave with us; they took their farewell of us through shining veils of tears, as if we were setting off on a journey into the underworld. Or perhaps they were crying at the thought of the destiny that awaited them in Bokhara. The farewell, at the foot of the red brick tower and the city walls, was a heavy one.

At last we climbed into the *hidjevas*. There were my parents, Boris and I, Bina and Tamhina, Bondy and Uljanow, and many others who were still unknown to me – the travails of the desert would rectify this, we would be introduced before we knew it. At the head of the caravan rode Hudaj-Verdy on his little donkey. Around his waist he had tied a rope which was threaded through the nose-rings of every one of our twenty-three camels. When the leading camel felt a tug in its nose it moved forwards and, in turn, tugged at the animal behind. But if the rope was to break or become detached from the ring, the camels would stop perplexedly and the whole caravan become immobile like a train without an engine.

Hudaj-Verdy cried out to his donkey, which moved off gingerly; the camels started also. Heavy and slow they strode with swaying rhythm, and their bells began a tinkling chorus. It was evening. The Tower of Death was gleaming once again, surrounded by its attendant Egyptian doves. The sound of wailing and crying voices was eventually drowned out by the bells of the caravan. While the red sun dyed the walls behind us, we set course for the desert and its trials.

14

Thirst

It was night, and our caravan was moving through the empty steppe of the Kara-Kul. Boris and I were sharing a camel. At every step the *hidjeva* jolted terrifically; we were making our first acquaintance with this ill-conceived implement of torture. We had not yet developed a technique for avoiding the discomfort of such a contraption, and hence we were thrown from side to side. It has been said that novices of desert travel suffer from seasickness, or something akin to it, but this has always struck me as an inaccurate analogy. The torture of the *hidjeva* is more excruciating: the continuous jolts invade the well-being of the entire body. My very intestines seemed tangled up, and I was amazed that my brain had not been disengaged from its fastenings.

Under these conditions it was impossible to sleep. I tried in vain to discover a rhythm in the camel's gait, and at last found an explanation. At the bottom of our *hidjevas*, underneath the wadded blankets, we had packed a thick layer of parsley. The camels, having caught the enticing smell, could have no rest until the delicacy had been eaten up; thus, at every step, our camel would lunge at the greenery protruding through the slats of the *hidjeva* in front. As soon as the supply of feed was exhausted, the caravan slowed down and became more rhythmic.

Towards midnight, just as we were going through a hamlet, our unfortunate beast put its foot into a pit. Before we knew it we were flung to the ground, and our camel was on its side. My *hidjeva* was tossed into the air and came crashing down over my head. But Boris was dashed against the road. We rushed up to him, still slumped in his shattered *hidjeva*, thinking that he was dead. However unlikely it seemed, we found him to be asleep; only with some determined shaking could he be roused.

There was no time to mend the *hidjevas*. Instead, Boris and I had to walk until six in the morning when we stopped for breakfast. I was so exhausted that I fell asleep and missed the bread and tea. At ten o'clock I woke up just as we were remounting. I climbed into my repaired *hidjeva*. A few hundred metres back I could see the Jewish caravan, also beginning to move after the morning halt. I counted up to fifty camels, the majority of them heavily loaded with fur. It was an imposing sight although, as we later realised, the merchants would keep their distance from us throughout the journey.

I curled up in my *hidjeva*, rested my chin against my knees, and determined to arm myself with patience. The heat intensified. Our driver had promised that by morning we would be safely at the oasis of Kara-Kul – but the sun had already climbed high, and we had not a single drop of water with us. As previously arranged, we were going to buy the driver's waterskins in Kara-Kul, and load them on to some spare camels brought for that purpose.

'Hudaj-Verdy! How much further to Kara-Kul?' my father cried.

'*Bir tasch!*' the driver said, without turning around.

The air trembled over the steppe; it was like being in an oven. Our thermometers showed 48 degrees

95

Reamur. The sweat was trickling down our faces, and our heads ached beneath insubstantial silk turbans. Our kaftans or *khalat*s were far too thin, and gradually we began to understand why desert people wore sheepskin hats and padded *khalat*s. My mother had put on a wide-rimmed panama hat, but it was so badly affected by the heat that it fell to pieces at the merest touch. My mouth and throat were dry as tinder, and the heat seemed to restrict even my breathing. Red balls were dancing before my eyes; from time to time, the hazy air hanging over the torched steppe was transformed into heavenly cascades of water. I saw white fields of snow, shimmering glaciers, the water came rushing towards me in great breaking waves, murmuring brooks, freshly running water – water – water. I put my hands over my eyes. Was I going mad? A glance at Boris made me want to retract my weakness. His lips were tightly pressed together, and his feverish gaze was directed at the far horizon. His whole being spoke of intense, compressed determination. I quelled my moans.

Towards evening our caravan crossed into a territory where the air was suffused with salt, and before too long our lips and tongues were covered in a bitter residue. And still there was not a single sign of life – not so much as a blade of grass, let alone a tree. Everything living had been burnt to death under the white sky.

My brain began to black out, and I remembered a fond expression from my adventure books: 'crazed with thirst . . .' Nor was I the only one to feel this way. Voices raved in the stillness, cursing our caravan, railing at our unscrupulous driver and calling for damnation to descend from the fiery heavens over his miserable being. All this suffering had been caused by his falsehoods – just to give him the opportunity of a paltry gain on his old waterskins! But Hudaj-Verdy did not as much as turn his head. Quiet and aloof he rode on on his donkey, keeping his evangelical brow high and proud. Even my father, usually the very model of self-control, began to wail as if he were out of his mind, 'I've got a good mind to put a bullet in his head!'

In the midst of all this, a stranger's voice began to utter the most hideous Turki oaths. What our importuning had failed to do, these wild curses achieved at once. The driver reined in his donkey and the caravan came to a halt. The furious cries had come from a man in the ranks behind us. I turned around and saw a strange sight indeed: a big black umbrella held aloft over a *hidjeva* where a woman sat with her husband, the latter bellowing with all his might.

As soon as the caravan stopped, he jumped off his camel; his wife, to re-establish the balance of the platform, had to fling herself across the camel's hump. She looked like a tightrope walker, balancing there with a leg in each box, holding up the umbrella. Under different circumstances it would have been a humorous sight, but my attention was diverted by the husband, who came storming along the caravan towards Hudaj-Verdy. He was an aberration of nature, a weird vision straight from a pirate novel by Robert Louis Stevenson. He limped terribly, so that every step was a monstrous lunge to the right. One of his eye-sockets was empty, and one hand was graced with a single remaining finger. The left arm was atrophied and hung limply by his side. This apocalyptic vision hurtled up to Hudaj-Verdy, and poured insults over the latter, who merely smiled insolently and repeated, '*Bir tasch . . .*' He looked as if he had never heard of a thing called thirst! He probably had a stomach like a camel.

The midget made a frenzied run back to the Jewish caravan, and initiated some heated negotiation with the drivers regarding the rental of a horse. Within minutes he was galloping past us, screaming at us with full voice, in Russian, 'I shall get water for us . . .' He rode away like a madman, and was soon gone. None of us knew who this incredible man was, but we found out that he was an Armenian by name of Oboljanz. He was among that number of hangers-on who had joined our caravan without as much as introducing themselves to my father. As it turned out, we would have ample opportunity to acquaint ourselves with Oboljanz; and it has to be said that the experience would be none too pleasant.

Evening approached without noticeable coolness. The sun was like a red iron ball over the horizon. We had gone waterless for twenty-two hours. Hypnotised, we stared towards the point on the horizon where Oboljanz had vanished. The sun was dancing in a thousand shattered fragments before our feverish eyes. Perhaps Oboljanz had gone mad? Or would he return with a big clay pot of cool water? No one had energy even for a complaint, or a moan. Mouths hung open limply, and our lungs took sporadic, panting gulps of hot air. The *hidjeva* rattled from side to side. My blood seemed to make a curious sound as it dragged itself through my veins, and the camel-bells pricked my eardrums like sharp needles.

At first I thought Oboljanz was a mirage when he reappeared on the horizon. He approached us at speed, waving with his good arm. As he came closer I could see his radiant face. 'Soon . . . soon you'll have water,' he bellowed. 'We'll be there in half an hour, forty-five minutes at the most. I left instructions with them to pump up as much water as they could. They wouldn't let me borrow a vessel, but very soon you'll be at the oasis, my friends . . .' His words ran through the caravan like an electric current. Our hopes reawakened. Shortly we saw the first trees silhouetted against the evening sky where the sun had set. If we had had the

98

energy we would have dismounted and run for it. Even the camels speeded up, as if sensing the proximity of water. And the driver's donkey hurried its steps, but this was due to Hudaj-Verdy poking his dagger into a kopeck-sized wound in the poor beast's neck. The practice was customary in these parts, as donkeys soon became impervious to kicks and blows. Tormenting an open wound always quickened their gait. And, after all, why should Hudaj-Verdy show his donkey mercy when he had shown none to us?

The trees rose up, soon we saw the contours of the huts, and within fifteen minutes the camels were congregating around a well; we dismounted and with weak tottering steps made our way to the long rows of filled clay vessels. With shaking hands we raised the water to our cracked and bloody lips, and felt the blessed liquid running down our parched throats and streaming over faces, breasts, hands. All our longing was stilled. This was an intoxicating drink provided for wretched, suffering people by some mild and provident god. It was water – water – water!

15

The Golden Road

As soon as we had extinguished our thirst and rested a short while, my father had Hudaj-Verdy brought before him. He ordered him to account for his behaviour. How could an experienced man, many times a leader of caravans between Bokhara and Kara-Kul, sanction the mistake of setting off without a drop of water? And how could he so falsely have informed us that we would arrive at the oasis by morning? Had he really let us thirst for twenty-two hours for the sake of the revenue on the sale of his waterskins?

'Are you really such a faithless human being, Hudaj-Verdy?' But Hudaj-Verdy smiled blithely, tilted his head, and fixed us with his inscrutable, evangelical gaze. Before too long it became clear that he had other faces too for he was soon involved in a brawl with Oboljanz. They screeched and lunged and parried with all the ferocity of a pair of rival cockerels. We deduced, without too much difficulty, that their dispute was connected with the affair of the waterskins. Apparently, the shrewd Oboljanz had approached Hudaj-Verdy to ask if he could have free passage with the caravan in return for a first-class business proposal. When Hudaj-Verdy signalled his interest, Oboljanz had expounded the devious scheme. My father was to be tricked into deferring his purchase of new waterskins in Bokhara, and persuaded to buy the second-hand ones in Kara-Kul. This would leave our driver with a fine profit.

Hudaj-Verdy, with loud insistence, was now making it perfectly clear to Oboljanz that free passage had only been granted as far as Kara-Kul. One bandit had double-crossed the other! My father, on hearing this, flew into a fit of unbridled rage, and matters might have ended in tragedy if my mother had not thrown herself into the fray, and placed herself between him and the two men. Oboljanz was brandishing both a revolver and a knife, for he had no other reply to my father's judicious accusations. However, Oboljanz was – for better or for worse – part of the caravan, and it was imperative to make as much use of him as possible. If we were to have any success at all, it was vital to maintain solidarity.

We had estimated that the journey to Merw would take eight days, but allowing for Sart notions of time and space, we were resigned to at least ten days in the desert. Further preparations were made during our time in Kara-Kul, and all the members of the caravan were assembled for a meeting. A *natschalnik* was chosen to see to the food stores, and another to secure ample quantities of water. One man was given the task of amassing fuel, while an orderly was assigned the responsibility of organising nightwatchmen and sentries even by day. This last duty befell the Czech officer, Bina. Oboljanz was to serve as interpreter during any exchanges with Sarts. Finally, a cook and kitchen assistant were chosen. I had the honour of the latter post, which consisted mainly of scrubbing pots and plates (owing to the scarcity of water, only sand could be used; I acquired formidable skills in this area, and can testify to the efficacy of desert sand, which far surpasses most modern scouring powders).

During our three days in Kara-Kul we were courted

by queues of the most enchanting boys and girls, as beautiful as any I had ever seen, who brought us the necessary provisions. They sold us chickens, cucumbers and melons, accepting gladly our Nikolai banknotes (still, at this time, in circulation) and silver coins from Bokhara. It was a pleasure to watch these accomplished children at work. Flour was the one thing they could not supply. It could only be obtained in a village situated a fair day's march away.

I wandered at will in Kara-kul. The village consisted of little more than ten mud huts and a few low buildings housing the camels. The dwellings were surrounded by mulberry trees, and there was an abundance of succulent berries in the leafage. The inhabitants seemed to be of mixed Arabic and Sart lineage. The men were tall and graceful, with charismatic features like those of Hudaj-Verdy. They did not even walk like men in Samarkand or Bokhara – hastily or with a slouch; rather they strode forward with a proud bearing and lordly composure. My mother was permitted to visit the women, who were at all times kept hidden from illegitimate admirers. She told me that they were as beautiful as the day itself. They wore nothing but long white garments which resembled nightgowns. Their hair was oiled with camel fat, and kept permanently in about thirty little plaits, each of them shining as if enamelled and decorated at its tip with a silver coin or tiny bell. But she also visited a hut which had been completely vacated, without as much as a stick of furniture or a single cooking implement. At the centre of the room lay a woman in her mid-thirties, her hands and feet bound by a strong rope. Unconscious and mortally ill, she had been left in this state to meet with her Maker. Hudaj-Verdy crouched at the entrance to the hut; he mumbled his prayers while ritually 'washing his face' with sand. When the sick woman – one of his wives – died towards evening, Hudaj-Verdy immediately jumped up and made a few jokes as if nothing had happened. Perhaps he had many more wives, younger and more beautiful.

But where the loss of a wife failed to rob him of his composure, Oboljanz could certainly claim greater success. Hardly an hour passed without some fleeting row between these two estimable gentlemen. Oboljanz simply could not forget that for once he was playing the role of dupe. By the end of the three days, he was firing shots close to the ears of our driver. This was the final straw. Hudaj-Verdy presented himself before my father and explained with unimpeachable dignity that he could not work for such a dog as Oboljanz, nor lead him through the desert. He offered instead to provide us with another driver, and introduced us to his uncle, Jamud-Aka. The latter was a man of about fifty years; thankfully, he did not have the misleading evangelical features of his nephew. His face radiated a steely resilience, and his sharp eyes inspired an instant confidence. He seemed to be all-seeing. In fact, I named him 'the Falcon'. As he straddled his donkey and made the sign for the caravan to move, there was a tangible feeling of optimism amongst us.

Finally, then, we were on the move. The first ten miles went pleasantly enough, but suddenly my father discovered five or six hair-thin jets of water escaping from each of the waterskins carried by the front three camels. He became extremely agitated, and asked Oboljanz what this could mean.

The Armenian answered with a malicious grin, 'It simply means, Mr Bank Manager, that Hudaj-Verdy's old waterskins are leaky and quite useless . . . but then as Mr Bank Manager bought them himself, he cannot blame anyone else . . .'

'That is quite correct. On the other hand, I had

no idea that I was dealing with crooks,' my father retorted.

'Are you calling me a crook . . . ?'

'We can talk about that some other time. First of all we have to deal with this question of the waterskins. Do you think these skins will last out the journey?'

Oboljanz shouted something to Jamud-Aka. The latter got off his donkey, whereupon the whole caravan came to an abrupt halt. Carefully he examined the waterskins, and then nodded at my father. There was such confidence, such assurance in this little nod, that all our fears were put to rest at once.

Something so empty and dead, so unvaried and hopeless, I had never envisaged until I saw the panorama of this landscape. Not the smallest green thing could be seen; the sun touched the sand so that it glowed – as glittering and merciless as gold was this way that lay ahead. This, for the first time, was the true desert. This was the 'golden road to Samarkand'. Eternally it stretched before me like some sea petrified by a mighty genie.

In places I noticed the withered remains of saksaul elms, which until February have leaves but by May are burnt to cinders. Their roots extend deep underground and are a welcome source of fuel. One such bush can keep a fire burning for a whole night. At the beginning of our passage we found the saksaul elm without any difficulty, yet as we penetrated the interior it became rarer. Our fires had to be nurtured with camel dung. The thermometer was soon showing 50–55 degrees Reamur at midday. We sweated profusely in the thick coats and fur hats purchased in Kara-Kul, but suffered less from the sun than we had previously done in flimsy silk turbans. Furthermore, the sweating helped regulate our body temperature. At every halt we drank ten cups of tea or more, but the beneficial effects never lasted for long.

104

Naturally, small cliques formed around separate camp-fires. My family associated with Bondy and the two Czech officers. Together we groaned in the heat, and amused ourselves by scrutinising the coterie of Oboljanz. One of the Czech officers had heard of Oboljanz in Taschkent. The Armenian, it turned out, was not fleeing the Bolsheviks; he was simply a common criminal, wanted for the murder of an old uncle. Obviously, he and his wife had brought with them the gains of this terrible crime. It was an unwholesome feeling having a cut-throat in our midst, although, sad to say, he could be no worse than Karamatilla. He was, however, a good deal uglier. This, we decided, was as it should be: a murderer should look hideous like Oboljanz, so that his neighbours could take note of him. Oboljanz and his wife had brought with them a tatty little man who we discovered to be a nephew, cast in the same ignoble form as his uncle. These three always kept themselves to themselves. Oboljanz looked most comical when he was sheltering with his wife under the skeleton of her black umbrella, long since crumbled by the sun but ingeniously repaired with a thick blanket. This contraption was the object of much professional jealousy until we hit on the idea of resting two *hidjevas* against one another, and laying a ceiling of blankets over the top. When the tea was made, we usually boiled eggs by simply putting them in the sand for a few minutes. Another clique consisted of the driver and his four helpers – all of them Sarts, responsible for the loading, feeding, saddling and watering of the camels. These four men walked on foot alongside the caravan, and had an immense strength and stamina. How else could they walk all day on a surface where the whole foot sank down into the fine sand?

The Jewish caravan never had anything to do with us. If our caravan stopped, the Jews did likewise at a good

105

distance. However thirsty they might be, they never once tried to overtake us on the final approach to a well, but always waited until we had slaked our thirst. Even in the desert, the Jews would not forget that they were a people who had to draw the shortest straw!

After two days we reached the first oasis, Daina-Kuduk. Its water was as salty as the ocean, and drinking it made one thirstier than before. Happily, our skins were still not emptied of the waters of Kara-Kul; but we had to be prudent as at the next well the water was said to be completely unfit for human consumption on account of its salinity.

At Daina-Kuduk we met a man who was driving a herd of a few hundred sheep to market in Bokhara. To get a bit of variety in our diet, we bought and slaughtered one of his animals. Four men held it down, and then Jamud-Aka drove his sharp dagger into its throat. Suddenly I seemed to see Karamatilla being slaughtered before my very eyes, and I ran away with tears streaming down my cheeks.

16

A Swedish Princess in the Desert

At nights we kept a strong blaze burning in the middle of the camp, and we slept close to it, wrapped in thick quilts to ward off the night's bitterness. The desert sky was loaded with a bright scattering of stars, but we were unable to lose ourselves in the sublimity of it all. The tormenting lice brought us down to earth. These parasites were synonymous with desert travel. While on the move, rattling along in the *hidjevas*, our bodies were less receptive to their torture. Yet as soon as we stopped they were upon us; both Sarts and camels were riddled with lice, so it was a hopeless endeavour to try to protect oneself against this indignity. Their bites caused a rash so irritating that soon our legs were, more or less, like bloody scabs. The Sarts seemed to be immune to the lice. We, in marked contrast, felt their little jaws so keenly that sometimes we cried out aloud.

At three in the morning, when only a slight blushing foretold the coming of our great enemy the sun, we sometimes felt a cool morning breeze; merely the intimation of coolness was enough to produce a rapturous shiver along the spine. Soon after, we would be on our way. Already by seven o'clock, the air would be so hot that we were reluctant to draw it into our lungs! Every day was hotter than its predecessor. For this reason, we increasingly had to travel by night. Frequently, our thermometer touched

59 degrees Reamur at noon. Our faces were flayed and burnt, our lips were bleeding. Between twelve and four in the afternoon we rested while the worst heat scorched the desert. The camels, undeterred, wandered in search of thistles, whose sharp thorns did not in the least give offence to their tongues. From time to time the Sart drivers fed their beasts on compressed oil cakes, and this – to my regret – caused the most repulsive breath. As soon as the caravan stopped, insects approached from all directions. There were beetles of all descriptions, and a lot of little crawling winged things whose names we did not know. While moving, we never saw them. I never ceased to wonder where these little beings came from, and how they knew of our coming. Within a few hours of setting up camp, the dung beetles were disposing of camel droppings, rolling them into balls and burying them.

I was often assigned guard duty, and to this end was given a cumbersome rifle which dwarfed me very convincingly. I suppose that my twelve-year-old figure would not have induced any great terror in the hearts of our enemies. I endured the pitiless sunlight, all the colours of the spectrum dancing before me. I put the rifle in the sand and sat down to concentrate on the small lizards that were darting around my feet. They were wonderful creatures, their skin camouflaged to coincide with the sand, their movements incalculably quick. Sometimes they stopped to stare at me with great surprise – for humans did not figure in their world – and the next instant burrowed into the sand and disappeared. Even when I put down the rifle, I never actually fell asleep. With smarting eyes I stood at my post, but sometimes, alas, I sat.

Our diet very rarely consisted of meat. We encountered no herdsmen or caravans. Our sustenance was reduced to rice, fat, bread and tea. Even the sugar supply was exhausted, and our cups of tea became remarkably dull. Bondy carried a bottle of some herbal extract, and he enlivened our bowls of tea and our hearts with a few drops of the tincture. As soon as we had broken camp and moved on, the jackals trotted in from their hiding places, and fought over any remains. Along our road lay the skeletons of horses, donkeys and camels, all polished by the sand until chalk white; in the moonlight these bones shone ghoulishly.

Our supply of rice and flour was carried by four pack mules. They were fed sparingly with a few handfuls of hay per day, and as the journey progressed they became thin as rakes, and lazy in the extreme. They developed an astonishing resilience to the beatings they received; in the end, the only remedy for their obstinacy was to tether them behind the camels and thus almost drag them onwards. Jamud-Aka rode his ass and poked its round wound with the tip of his knife, but his efforts were in vain, for the caravan made slow progress. From the rear of the caravan there was constant shouting from Oboljanz, imploring us, in his own charmless way, to quicken the pace. Already on the fourth day, he had extended his repertoire by sneaking over to the Jewish caravan and stealing some hay for his nephew's horse. The Jews immediately made complaints to my father, who had to settle matters as well as he could. Unfortunately, the nephew of Oboljanz was another worthless dolt whose horse had to be kept supplied with water – this also procured by Oboljanz from the Jewish caravan. The pilfering eventually led to fighting between the Jews and Oboljanz. Boris and my father had to intervene with drawn guns before peace could be re-established.

But this nephew could also steal in his own right; Boris caught him red-handed just as he was about to appropriate an emergency supply of sugar. This earned him a sound beating. On the following evening he presented himself at our campfire as if nothing had happened. Probably he felt that yesterday's dishonour had to be redressed.

He bowed, slammed his heels together, and said to my mother, in a rather pretentious tone,

'Good evening, honourable lady. Will you allow me to present myself? My name is Kalantarow – Dr Kalantarow.'

'Are you a doctor?' my father asked.

'No . . . I'm a field surgeon. But it is more or less the same thing . . .'

'It is remarkable that your name is Kalantarow,' said my father, 'you an Armenian and all! I happen to know a prominent Jew in Bokhara with the very same name, and he assures me that it is unique to his family . . .'

Our visitor looked ill at ease; he mumbled something ill-defined into his beard. Then he turned his attention to me. I was sitting bare-torsoed by the fire, doing what I always did in the evenings – ridding my shirt of lice.

'Oh these horrible lice!' he burst out with disgust. 'The other day I found no less than seven of them in my shirt . . .' His remark produced a sudden jollity around the campfire. We laughed with all the strength left in us. The Armenian glared at us suspiciously. Had he said something unsuitable in front of the European lady? Seeing that our hilarity increased at the sight of his perplexed face, he went away in humiliation. How could he have known that I had just thrown a fat louse into the fire, with the words; 'That must be the two hundredth one tonight . . .' To mention a mere seven puny lice seemed to us the very height of affectation! The desert sand quickly smooths away the veneer of European manners.

On the sixth day rolling hills loomed up before us, and within hours we were picking our way through magnificent high dunes. Often we had to dismount from our camels and clamber up the sandy mountains; their slopes were steep, and our feet were swallowed in the gluttonous sand. The evening sun toyed with our shadows, pitching them against the varying gradients of the dunes; at every step, the elongated violet shadows of the camels grew smaller or greater, or shifted to a deep blue. On the ninth day, with great relief, we emerged from the belt of dunes and found flat terrain.

The slow strides of the camels, the soundless footfalls of great feet against the soft sand! The endless ochre sea, the tinkling bells and braying donkeys! Mercifully, the distance between camels was enough to drown out most of the mad whispers that came to our lips. During the long marches, there was only one constant thought in our minds, one constant image: water!

By now we are on the tenth day, and our provisions are almost exhausted. Our driver, at the outset, predicted a journey of some nine days at most. We have only bread and rice to eat. Probably we are not even half way. Soon we shall have to cross the Amudarja River; our minds are full of pictorial reveries of rivulets and rock pools and running water. Maybe we will be able to buy some food at the Amudarja. The driver has said that we will meet with an oasis, and then another five-hour march will take us to the Amudarja. We sit, staring fixedly at the horizon, hoping to see just one green, living tree. Soon I sink into a stupor.

A hand shakes me roughly by the arm. It is Boris, who addresses me with an insistent, almost wild voice. 'I can't endure this any more. You have to tell me about something, so we have something to think about . . .'

'I don't have any strength.'

'Yes you do. Tell me a story so the time passes more quickly – and let's forget about all this! You promised

111

that you'd tell me about the Swedish princess . . .' If anything can make us forget the trials of this caravan, it is the memory of her . . . I begin to speak.

'A few years ago I was on my way home from the Conservatory in Saratoff at the end of the term, and I'd passed Samara. I was sitting in my third-class carriage thinking about nothing in particular when a very smart officer came walking along the aisle. When he saw me sitting there by myself, he seemed to feel sorry for me. I could see that he was a little drunk. But he nodded very kindly at me.

'"Good day, my little boy . . . are you travelling all alone? All alone? To Samarkand? That's a very long way for a little urchin like you. And you've got a violin, I see . . . are you a musician?"

'"Yes," I told him, "I'm a musician. I've just played my examination piece at a student gala held in honour of Saffonow. He thanked me and kissed my forehead. Now I'm going home to my parents . . ."

'"If you want to, you can come and sit with me in the first class. I've got a spare seat."

'"First class!" I burst out. "With silk curtains and velvet sofas?"

'"That's right," he laughed. "Silk and velvet and no fleas . . ."

'Before he had time to change his mind, I took my cap and violin and said goodbye to the farmer who had been my travelling companion. The officer carried my knapsack. With barely contained excitement I followed him down the corridor. He had a sumptuous compartment. Clean, spacious, and soft couches to sit on! And he was so kind that I was not the least bit afraid of him.

'"Would you like some champagne?" he asked. Of course I wanted champagne! He pulled out a flat suitcase from under the divan. Boris, can you guess what was in it? Can you?' Boris shakes his head. 'There were six bottles of champagne, boxes of chocolate, juicy big pears, apples, and little decorative boxes of Russian marmalade. I thought my eyes were going to pop out of my head, and I couldn't help salivating, but the officer just laughed and said, "Take what you want . . ."'

'I helped myself to the biggest piece of chocolate and the grandest pear I could find, and then he uncorked one of the bottles and filled two glasses. I thought it tasted like the most delicious lemonade and immediately asked for another glass. He just laughed and filled my glass again. I devoured the pear, juice was running down my chin, and I took bites at the chocolate. After my second glass I thought everything had become so marvellous that I began to laugh as heartily as the officer. He topped up my glass for the third time, but I couldn't drink any more, even though it tasted so good and fizzed so exquisitely . . .'

Boris pinches my arm suddenly, and cries out, a little peeved, 'Be so kind as not to speak of drink all the time . . . what's happened to the Swedish princess?'

'Take it easy. She's coming in a minute. Anyway. I was beginning to feel tired so I lay back. "Uncle, now I want to sleep," I said, but he looked dissatisfied with this.

'"You can't sleep now! It's one o'clock in the afternoon! It's just not done! You're going to play for me. You told me that Saffonow himself kissed your brow. What did you play for him?"

'"Accolay's Concerto in A minor . . ."

'"That'll be fine. We'll have it in A minor then . . ."

'And with this, he brought down my violin from the luggage rack, and I began to play. My fingers felt very peculiar, and the champagne seemed to be bubbling in my body. I kept playing. It was a rigid, very classical

113

piece, and I could see that the officer found it boring. He stopped me, tugging at my arm, and asked me to play something beautiful, something sensitive to make one cry. So I played Braga's Serenade for the kind officer, who by now was fairly intoxicated. He lay back on the divan, lit a cigarette, and really did start to cry. When I put down the violin he thumped my back and said that I had played better than all the world's virtuosos put together.

'"You're going to travel with me," he said.

'"Where to?"

'"To the Swedish princess."

'"Does Uncle really know a princess?"

'"Oh yes, you can count on it . . ."

'"A real princess?"

'"As real as they come. Quite so! And you're going to travel with me, and play your violin for her . . ."

'This adventure was becoming more and more enchanting by the minute. First-class carriage, champagne, chocolate, and a real princess! I agreed to his plan, clambered on to the sofa, and fell asleep immediately. When I woke up at six in the evening, the officer was having a shave.

'"Good morning, little man," he said cheerfully. "Now we should have some supper, followed by a game of blackjack and other pleasant pursuits . . ." Shaving concluded, he fetched another trunk, from which he produced bread, caviare and schnapps. I partook of the first two, but when the officer politely offered me a glass of the latter, I declined, explaining that champagne was more to my taste. He laughed and told me that the champagne had to be saved for the princess. Then he started to tell me about her. I couldn't quite grasp what he was saying. He said that she was travelling incognito with the Swedish Red Cross, and that she was giving food and presents to

114

German and Austrian prisoners of war interned in the big camps.

'"But remember you mustn't call her princess."

'"What's her name then?"

'"Elsa. You'll make her so happy if you play for her. In five or six hours we'll be in Totzkoje, where there's a massive prison camp. That's where we'll find her. I've been in Samara to stock up on essential supplies. I'm her assistant and her interpreter, you see. She also has a full retinue travelling with her, of course: a doctor, a Swedish chamber lady, and a cook . . ."

'My heart pounded with anticipation. A real, living princess! I envisaged her in a golden crown, dragging a mantle of ermine and crimson velvet. It would be like the fairy tales of Hans Christian Andersen. I wanted to ask whether she might present me with a gold medal, but I stopped myself in time, feeling that the question might be insolent.

For the rest of the evening we played blackjack, and by ten o'clock I was asleep again. At midnight I woke up. The officer was standing over me, shaking me by the arm and whispering urgently, "We'll be in Totzkoje Sel in a few minutes . . . with Princess Elsa." Two ladies were waiting for us on the platform. One of them was short, dark, and kind-looking. The other was tall, straight-limbed and blonde. She was smiling at us with the most blindingly white teeth. Beside them stood a corpulent gentleman and a servant. The officer presented me to the gathering, but he spoke English, and so I couldn't understand. The strangers laughed appreciatively, and they all shook me by the hand. I didn't attach too much importance to them. I was frantically scanning the surroundings for a glimpse of my princess. In the end I tugged at the officer's sleeve and entreated him to tell me where the princess was.

'"Be quiet!" he said. "She's the blonde lady with the

115

red cross on her arm . . ." Alas, what disappointment for my poor heart, which had entertained hopes of enchantments and fairytales. By God, all I wanted to do was grab my violin and knapsack, board the train again, even find my third-class compartment. But at that instant, just as I looked around, I saw the train disappearing around the bend, trailing a plume of smoke.

'There was nothing for it but to go with the company; we walked across the sleepers to an ordinary third-class wagon, which served as a princess's travelling castle. The two central compartments had been joined together into a large dining area. There was a table with many chairs; and on the table, a sumptuous feast. I was given a seat next to the blonde lady; I was still hurting from the disappointment, it has to be said, and on top of all this I was very tired. But everything looked brighter as soon as I began talking with the charming 'Princess Elsa' – whenever I addressed her by her title, there was an intense merriment around the table. She filled my glass with milk, she served me food, and was kind to me in every conceivable way. Her long blonde hair was tied in a swelling soft knot against the nape of her neck, and she smiled at me with teeth as bright as sunlight. She was obviously a true princess after all; how else could she be so beguilingly beautiful?

'After the meal she asked me to play some music. By now it must have been three in the morning; the dawn chorus was beginning outside, and all the windows were flung wide open against the brightening sky. I played Accolay's concerto. My princess listened very attentively. When I came to the end, she kissed me. "Now I'll get the gold medal," I thought, but all I got was the kiss. After that I played the serenade by Braga, and I was a little disappointed, I think, because she liked it – as for myself, I had never been too fond of the

116

sentimental pieces. I can't remember what else I played. In the end I fell asleep at the table, and when I came to, I was lying in a comfortable bed in a nightshirt. When the officer told me that the princess herself had undressed me and put me to bed, I was acutely embarrassed. Everyone had slept in the railway carriage. Later on, Elsa came to fetch me. We were going fishing in a lake full of waterlilies; she presented me with a little fishing rod, but I wanted to pick a lily flower for her, and almost fell into the water. She managed to grab me by the shirt-tails. We didn't speak very much. I was just looking at her, admiring her beauty. She laughed when I said, "*Schönes Fraulein, Schöne blonde Haare! Schöne Prinzessin!*" These German phrases were all I could muster.

'On the same day, a telegram was despatched to my parents in Samarkand. It caused a great sensation, Boris. And it went like this: "ENTERTAINING MYSELF WITH THE SWEDISH RED CROSS DELEGATION. SHALL ARRIVE IN TWO DAYS."

'These two days were sweet, spent in the company of my princess, who was waiting for permission from the Russian government to enter the prisoner-of-war camp. It was not so far away, with all its crowded horrors; and yet, here I rowed with her on a lake, picked waterlilies, and played my violin to keep her entertained. Two worlds, one idyllic and one of suffering, situated together with no margin between them. I had my diary with me, and she wrote a few lines in it. It was very difficult to part with her. Everyone was down at the station, waving me off. The kind, dark-haired lady, whose name was Fru Linder, gave me a jar of marmalade. My princess gave me twenty-five roubles, a first-class ticket home, and as a keepsake, her very own little embroidery scissors of silver with gilded tips. She kissed me farewell,

117

and as the train pulled away, she cried: "*Komm nach Stockholm . . .*"'

'Be still a moment,' Boris cries suddenly, as he grips me excitedly. He has been listening attentively throughout, but now he is pointing at the skyline. I follow the direction of his unwavering finger. Something is standing in relief against the sky. The oasis. The green trees of hope are there. And so the memory of this woman has shortened the agonising hours in the desert for two suffering people, just as, in the past, her name brought solace to many hundreds of thousands of people.

But I did not know about her deeds then, as I do now. '*Komm nach Stockholm,*' she had cried. Little did I know, as we hurried towards the impending oasis, that my way would indeed lead to this city of her homeland, and that twenty years later I would once again shake her hand – set eyes on the face of my princess. In my book she wrote a few lines that had been the guiding stars for her family over many generations. They can also be seen as a tribute to her own life, and I hereby set them down in honour of her many deeds; and in gratitude to her for imprinting my childhood with such an indelible memory:

> *Auf Worte nicht,*
> *auf Taten nur,*
> *beruht des Menschen Wert.**

---

* 'Not by words, only by deeds, can we affect the dignity of humanity.' Elsa Brändström-Ulick, active in Siberia on behalf of the Swedish Red Cross 1914–20. Established sanatoriums in Sachsen and Brandenburg. Emigrated to the USA in the 1930s when the Nazis came to power.

118

17

Bandits

It was almost other-worldly, after ten days in the desert, to find these vigorous green trees standing there as a symbol of the victory of life. There were sixteen of them, lithe and tall, casting a deep and cooling shade in which we rested during the hottest hours of the day. The anticipation of the river gave further pleasure to this lassitude. There was a dry spring in the oasis, and the Sarts inspected it to see if it would yield some water; when I heard loud yells, I rushed over to find them in hot contest with a lizard, both in size and appearance very much like a crocodile. Furiously it snapped at their legs, and they tried to defend themselves with wooden stakes, which the beast chewed to pieces like lengths of boiled asparagus. At last they killed it by wounding it in its one weak area: the eyes. In spite of its hide, thick as a crocodile's, it disintegrated within the hour, rotting quite away in the burning sun. The Turkmen call this monster the Kitschkinar.

With sadness we departed from our shade and beloved trees, but fresh joys lay in wait for us as we reached the Amudarja River by evening; the stars were already reflected in its waters when we threw ourselves down and stilled our thirst. The water was yellow with sediment, but for us it was pure nectar. We drank until our stomachs distended like balloons. Then we threw off our heavy filthy garments, and rushed into the river where we played like children. The Sarts remained on the shore, busily watering the camels; each one drained ten buckets. Following this, all the waterskins were replenished. Heavenly music lulled us to sleep that night: the gentle mumuring of the Amudarja. At five in the morning we began the crossing, overseen by twelve tall Chiwini, who looked spectacularly murderous – flashing eyes, metre-high fur hats, and broad knives in their belts. They did not hurry. Every time they took a load of camels and men across, they rested and drank tea. As a consequence, it took six hours to ferry our caravan, and thereafter the Jewish caravan, across in the flat barges. When I saw the Chiwini sitting between the hulls drinking tea and eating raisins, I could not resist the temptation. Timidly I approached and indicated that I wanted some. After all, for several days I had eaten nothing but rice and fat. The wildest of them grabbed a fistful and pressed it into my hand – but he fixed me with his eyes like a wild animal and let out a diabolical, guttural scream. Petrified I ran back to our camp, with the Chiwini's scream still echoing behind me.

Oboljanz was the only one who could communicate with them. He asked if they had any news from Merw. Was General Malleson still holding the town? The Chiwini said that they knew nothing about it. But they told him that Russian boats often passed, and that it would not be wise to light big fires at night, as this would alert the Bolsheviks. As soon as we had crossed the river, we continued into the desert. On the thirteenth day, Jamud-Aka halted the caravan. He scanned the horizon and shook his head anxiously. He claimed to have noticed something up ahead; however hard we stared, we could see nothing.

'Is it a caravan?' Oboljanz asked.

'No, not a caravan. It's not the smell of camels . . . the wind is full of horses. It is an evil sign . . .'

By nightfall we arrived at Sartandlj-Kuduk, a well which was marked on our maps. Its water was so bitterly salt that even the camels refused it. From the maps, however, we saw that Merw was now within a day's march. We tried to egg our driver on, but it proved impossible to make him move. He shook his head and announced that he would not continue. Oboljanz, resorting to a tried and tested formula, waved the revolver about, while the impetuous nephew ran behind Jamud-Aka and lashed out threateningly with a long whip. The rest of us entreated him with every device in our power; but it was all useless. Jamud-Aka remained motionless in the sand, calmly staring at the horizon.

Finally he condescended to explain the cause of his disquiet. Oboljanz translated for us. All day, Jamud-Aka had, as he put it, 'seen' the smell of horses. This had to mean that there were riders in the vicinity. Suddenly their scent had disappeared; up until that point they had been heading for us, and the smell had been getting stronger. When it disappeared it must mean that they had changed course. He was convinced that they were manoeuvring around us in a half-circle, planning to attack us in the rear as soon as the night came. Hence we had to prepare ourselves for an ambush by bandits. When Oboljanz translated this last sentence, he paled noticeably. But my father was not one to lose his head. 'Nonsense,' he said. 'We have a rifle, four revolvers, and a hand grenade. Surely this must be enough to earn the respect of a few riders. Counting the Jews we are more than fifty men. Tell Jamud-Aka that enough rubbish has been talked here . . . tell him that we're moving on!' After additional discussions, the driver eventually gave the order to his men; the camels were collected and loaded, and then we moved.

For the first time during this journey, thick clouds

121

began to pile up in the sky. When darkness fell it was so black that we could not even see the stars. Then the wind came like a whiplash, and soon the sand was flying mercilessly against our faces. The wind was hot, as if it had come straight out of an oven. Soon, I was yet again sinking into the eternal land of thirst. In my *hidjeva* I had a small clay pot, purchased from a herdsman; it held no more than the equivalent of a drinking glass of water, but I only took a few drops at a time, to moisten my lips. Such treasures had to be used sparingly. The caravan moved with uncharacteristic speed. Probably it was the fear of robbers that inspired the feet of Jamud-Aka. It still defies my understanding how he found his way through that night; it was dark as in a sack.

Just after midnight we heard the whinnying of horses and the gallop of a troop of riders. We listened as hard as we could, for it was impossible to see anything. Then from the Jewish caravan came the sound of shots and crying voices. Our caravan stopped, and the camels were settled into a circle, with their legs bound together so that they could not move. Inside this low wall of living flesh we lay down on the ground. The air was dense and heavy, sand was everywhere, but we stopped paying attention to such inconveniences. Now it was a matter of our lives. In the darkness, I fumbled back to my camel and felt in the *hidjeva* for my pot of water. It had gone. I crawled back to my father and lay down next to him.

'Are you afraid?' he asked. I pressed myself as close to him as I could. He was pressing my mother's hand in his; I could hear her sobbing. In his other hand he held mine. The revolver was propped up against my chest. It was so dark that we could not even see the contours of the camels in front of us. I could hear Bondy whispering with the Czech officers – a hurried military council, during which they decided who should take the rifle, and who should throw the grenade.

Oboljanz and his nephew started shouting with all their might, in the Sart dialect, 'Are you ready, comrades? Is the cannon loaded? Load the rifles! Are all the rifles loaded? Have you got the hand-grenades ready?'

They bellowed like this for several hours, with a few intervals. Mrs Oboljanz was less courageous. She banged her head against a *hidjeva* with an almighty crash, and screamed like a terrified bird. But Oboljanz drowned her voice with an inhuman burst of yelling. 'Get those hand-grenades out now . . . prepare yourselves . . . let's give those damned robbers something to think about!'

I don't know how long we had been lying there, in terror, when we heard another volley of shots. Then a rider came towards us at speed, crying for Oboljanz. Evidently he came from the Jewish caravan. He leapt over a camel's broad back, and breathlessly began to relate something to Oboljanz. He was so frightened that he could hardly speak, his voice choked on itself; Oboljanz had no time to translate the message. He told us, however, to make as much din as we could, to scream our defiance and disdain of the robbers, who were presently looting the merchants' caravan. He took the lead in this, screaming like a lunatic. It made a hellish discord! We hollered for as long as we could, and then we clasped hands and prayed and tried to make ready for death.

It was a horrible night. Oboljanz was moaning with terror, and his wife sounded like an animal. Most likely, their consciences were troubling them on the very eve of their demise. Dr Kalantarow was creeping about, hissing constant warnings: 'Look out, there they are! Can't you see their fur hats? Over there!

Get ready! Here they come . . .' His fear was contagious. Our nerves underwent a collective breakdown; we panicked at the merest movement of one of our camels' heads.

Even the most terrible night, it must be said, has a morning. At sunrise a few men from the Jewish caravan rode over to tell us of the night's events. Jamud-Aka had made an accurate guess. He had indeed observed some riders on the horizon. There were eight of them, fully armed, all of them in the service of the Emir of Bokhara. In fact, they were bearing a message for him when their acute noses had caught scent of us; immediately they had determined to raid us. And, as Jamud-Aka had described, they rode around us and attacked our rear. The Jewish caravan had caught the brunt of their attack. All gold and money was taken. When they started to loot the bales of merchandise from the pack camels, a Jewish driver had convinced them that these belonged to a well-armed Christian caravan up ahead. Another driver managed to escape on horseback. This was the man who had come to us in the night with news of the ambush.

When the robbers realised that he had gone to warn the powerful Christian caravan, they convened a hasty war-council, and thereafter made a quick escape, bearing the booty in ready cash. If we had been told of this at once, it would have saved us many anxious hours. But no one gave it any further thought! Our lives were saved, and soon we would be in Merw, the goal and reward for all our suffering.

Onwards, then! The sky was still wreathed in thick clouds, and this helped us to endure the next fourteen hours without water. When we reached our first well and hauled up the first bucket of water, it was found to contain the rotten head of a donkey. It stank. But

124

after fourteen hours without a drink, we attached no significance to this grisly find. Without exception we drank greedily of the water. Oddly enough, no one became ill. When we made tea, it was green and looked most unsavoury. Furthermore, it tasted bitter. A bitter drink on a bitter evening that we would never forget.

My father discovered Oboljanz in a passionate quarrel with Jamud-Aka.

'What's wrong now?' he demanded.

'Jamud-Aka won't take us to Merw, he says, because there are no Englishmen there, only a lot of Bolsheviks . . .'

My father listened carefully, thinking he had misunderstood. Oboljanz continued, 'Jamud-Aka says that he has known about this since the Amudarja River . . .'

'Why didn't he tell us before we crossed the river?'

'He says that he didn't find out until we had already crossed over to this side. The Chiwini wouldn't tell us until we'd paid them for the boats . . .'

'How can people be such swine!' cried my poor father, utterly desolate. And he charged at Jamud-Aka, and shook him furiously by the shoulders, shouting, 'You worthless misguided man, couldn't you have told us before, and saved us the pains of this terrible journey!' Jamud-Aka freed himself, and answered with a fair amount of aloofness, which was duly translated by Oboljanz.

'He explains that he has been engaged to take us to Merw, and whether there are Englishmen or Bolsheviks there it is no concern of his . . .' My father went pale with a deadly and silent fury. Boris stepped in between the two men.

'Is it possible that the driver has made a mistake?' he wondered.

125

Our translator began to remonstrate and gesture expressively with his hands – we could see that he too was becoming upset. He could barely speak, so overcome was he with anger. 'Jamud-Aka says that the Bolsheviks took Merw a whole month ago, and now he tells us! He knew about it in Kara-Kul when he led us into the desert . . .' Now it was Boris's turn to lose himself in legitimate anger. When the driver saw the united front of Oboljanz, my father and Boris, he wisely decided to make himself scarce. Despair, tears and powerless fury held sway in our camp. Hunger, thirst, suffering and deadly perils had all been endured for naught. Only a few kilometres away lay the city of Merw, with shady gardens and quantities of food and water. But for us, the city could promise nothing but certain death. He we stood, ready to collapse with incredulity, and all because of faithlessness and devilish greed in our fellow human beings.

But we wanted to live, and in view of this, there was only one thing to do: return the way we had come, back to Bokhara. We had to pray that this city had not yet fallen to the Reds, for then we would be doomed. Our stores of food were wholly depleted. Fourteen days the journey had taken us! How could we last through the rigours of another such journey? Oboljanz was told by the driver that we could purchase a quantity of rice at the Amudarja.

Within the hour, we were on our way back. We had starved, thirsted, and suffered the effects of heat until barely recognisable: our cheeks were sunken, our eyes set in deep hollows. Despairingly, we turned our weary eyes to the north. What destiny awaited us there? And so, into the desert we went once again, on swaying mounts. I bit my lips, but I could not contain my tears. I was only twelve years old.

126

Boris touched my arm. Through a veil of tears I looked at him, and he smiled his brave smile and pointed upwards. I looked. The first star was appearing in the vault of the night sky.

18

Bokhara Once More

Our supplies were almost exhausted, and we had to reach the Amudarja as quickly as possible to stock up on the necessary comestibles. To this end we pushed north with almost no rest. We slept two hours in the day, and only made halts to bake bread. The dough was kneaded together with rye and salt water, flattened into a cake; then simply covered in red-hot sand from under a fire. When fresh, the bread was edible. If not consumed at once, it became hard as stone – an excellent medium for breaking one's teeth.

A few days into this hurried jouney we met a shepherd, from whom we bought a few sheep. Almost before their carcasses were properly grilled, we fell on the meat like famished jackals, leaving nothing but a heap of polished bones. We crossed the Amudarja once more, further to the north this time, and were able to secure rice, bread and two sacks of flour, otherwise we would have been in serious trouble. My poor mother had been sorely tested by our misadventures, and she was in a terrible condition. An aged Sart of the Amudarja was overtaken by compassion. He gave her a boiled leg of chicken. She ate half of it, and handed the rest to me. I don't think I ever paid so much attention to a little morsel of food. Even the bone was gnashed to pieces, and the marrow greedily sucked out.

The thermometer daily touched 60 degrees Reamur.

Nerves were tight as bow-strings, close to breaking point. Irrational disputes would suddenly flare up and then die down without trace. The antagonists would stand there with clenched fists, then their arms would drop as they turned perplexedly away. There was no fight left in them.

On the eighth day of our retreat we encountered a sandstorm even more violent that its predecessor. Our tracks in the sand were instantly rubbed out, and in the morning we woke up under a blanket of sand half a metre thick. Cooking pots, food, and trunks, had to be dug up from drifts of sand. The rice I boiled that morning was crunchy between the teeth. All day, Jamud-Aka meandered across the dunes in search of the well that was supposed to lie along our way.

He plunged his hands deep into the sand, feeling for the camel dung that would indicate we were on the right path. Sand was whizzing about our ears, whipping against our tender faces. Whoever has not experienced it could never imagine the torture of such hour-long storms, when burning grains of sand inflame the face like fine needles, and sting beneath one's eyelids. From time to time, the storm tore up great pillars of sand which came towards us like tornados and drove terror into our camels. They bellowed hoarsely, and tried to break free. We doggedly held on to the sides of our *hidjeva*s, doing our best not to be tipped out. Then, on the following morning, we finally located Getschekran, the well we sought, and stilled our suffering with its bitter waters.

On the twelfth day we rode into Kara-Kul once again. The caravan had hardly stopped before Oboljanz threw himself at Hudaj-Verdy, who was waiting for us at the well. He was overpowered by the Armenian, who cursed him roundly for his leaking waterskins, and for his betrayal in allowing us to continue to Merw, whose

129

fate he had already known. But no words could move this bandit. He had had his payment, and that was the only thing that concerned him. His eyes were aloof, he smiled into his neatly trimmed beard; it was horrific to behold this mask of Christ-like goodness, and to know that its gentle features obscured a veritable devil.

Two days later we approached Bokhara, having gathered news from a passing caravan that the Emir was still in his capital. At least, then, some time remained for us to live. Hope reawakened in our breasts. At last the camels lay down by the city gates. Exhausted as we were, we ran as fast as our legs could carry us into the bazaar, to gorge on fruit, bread, meat and milk. In Scandinavia I have seen cows and calves released on to pasture after the long winter. I suppose that we were not unlike such exuberant cattle. It was the evening of 12 June. We had departed from Bokhara on 15 May. Our perilous journey had taken us twenty-eight long days, and all had been in vain! But on this June evening we did not think about our wasted efforts, for we still had hope.

Once again we took up occupancy of the little house next to the mosque. I slept with my parents in one room, while the other room was shared between Boris, the Czech officers Bina and Tamhina, and Uljanow the lawyer. We had no cooking utensils and we slept on the floor with just a quilt beneath us. Bondy had had enough, and he took a train to Samarkand, there to be reunited with his fiancée whom he had missed terribly. He was reconciled to a protracted, uneasy wait for the demise of the Bolsheviks.

Bina, Tamhina and Uljanow did not own a single rouble between them. Their resources had been wholly depleted by our first expedition. The Czechs claimed that they had contacts in Prague who would reimburse my father for all expenses incurred in their name.

Uljanow had no foreign friends, but he promised to make himself useful in all our endeavours.

Rumours still abounded in the Old City. In the Russian colony, people were outdoing each other with the extravagance of their claims, but of one thing we were all certain: Bokhara would soon be taken by the Reds; only the timing of their invasion, and not the certainty of it, was in doubt. Four rusty cannons stood in pathetic formation by the city gates. And the ragged companies of undisciplined soldiers would surely run away as soon as the Bolsheviks fired the first warning shots.

Hence, my father decided to set about organising a second caravan with no further delay. To avoid the necessity of travelling with the criminal Armenian clique, absolute secrecy had to be maintained. As for the destination and the date of our departure, he decided to wait for a moment of insight to inform our actions. At any rate, the murderous summer heat dissuaded Sart drivers from taking on our commission and the beginning of August would be the earliest time we could leave. A Russian engineer, who had been repairing the water system in the Emir's palace, told us that the royal harem, consisting of some 300 women, was fully prepared for flight. The palace courtyards were crowded with camels, fully loaded and saddled, day and night.

That propitious moment which my father had been awaiting was provided by destiny on an evening at the end of July. A woman with a black veil over her face appeared outside our house. She put a finger on her lips and hurried inside. Once the door was closed behind her, she threw off the veil and revealed herself as Bondy's fiancée. She whispered her message to us, anxiously listening for the sound of feet. She was now married to Bondy, whose ring she wore. She had entered Bokhara in the company of a Bolshevik, their

131

assignment to garner information for the sekretariat in Samarkand. She had got rid of her colleague by sending him to the home of a Bokhara Jew. She told us that the fall of Bokhara had been determined by the Soviet for the end of September. We were now at the end of July, and therefore had two months at the most to make our escape.

We should consider routing our caravan northwards to Kasalinsk and the Aral Sea, close to the territories held by Denikin's Army! This journey, she informed us, would cross the Kirghiz steppe and be less dangerous than our previous attempt for Merw, of which Bondy had told her. With good camels we could reach the Aral Sea in eight days.

'And now I must go . . . there are people waiting for me. If it becomes known that I have come to you, my life will not be worth much. Samarkand is a terrible place now, most of my friends have been murdered. I must go! May God grant that we meet again . . .'

My father immediately stepped up the pace of his preparations, and negotiated agreements with retailers and drivers. Most Sarts refused our assignment until the very end of August but, with the help of the merchant Kalantarow, we at last found a man willing to lead us, in two weeks' time, to the Aral Sea. Everything had been well prepared. New waterskins had been purchased, as well as thick blankets, sugar, rice, flour, fat, raisins and, for each of us, a clay water-pot to be carried in the *hidjeva*. We had also constructed sunscreens of wood and strengthened cloth. Our experiences on the road to Merw had taught us not to suffer again.

All that remained was to wait. We were soundly bored with the sameness of life in Bokhara. Every face in the bazaar was familiar to us, and the other Russians did little else but frighten us with horror stories; some of them knew we were planning another caravan, and they lovingly painted a picture of the Kirghiz as a bloodthirsty people, and the steppe as a charnel house. Human life meant nothing to the Kirghiz! We listened and kept silence. We had become hardened.

By seven in the evening the bazaar was empty, and the curfew began. An exception was made for the Bajrem festival, which lasted a whole week. The city's inhabitants took to the streets, and danced through the nights. Music and singing rebounded from every cranny, and lanterns and torches brightened the lanes. One could almost imagine that this was a city of joy and peace. At night, there were watchmen on the rooftops, beating out drum rolls to frighten away thieves. Many of them were virtuosos on their instruments, and could play three drums at once; nevertheless, it was unpleasant to be woken up by someone on the roof making a sudden noise.

Within the lanes and labyrinths of the Old Town, I discovered a large tank which went by the name of the Libikaus. This pool, a hundred metres square, was refilled fortnightly with water from the Zarawschan River. It was a murky indictment of the East's whole-sale ignorance of hygiene, although, ironically, it was intended for ritual cleansing as prescribed by the Koran. The first few days after being replenished, the water was passable; thereafter the level dropped, green scum floated on the surface, and there was a nasty stink. In this tank the Sarts washed their hands, feet and faces, as their beloved Koran ordered them to do. Here they gargled, here they spat, and here they drank to still their thirst. The Koran decrees that water is purified by merely turning it seven times in the hand. It would have been less serious if the people of Bokhara had been strikingly healthy and untainted! But even those with venereal diseases washed their bodies here, and many times one saw men with *trakom* (the Egyptian

133

eye affliction) rinse their purulent, running eyes in the very same water that, next to them, some blissful Sart was drinking.

The tank was obviously a source of pestilence, but to say so would have been dangerous – throwing into doubt the infallibility of the Koran. Many people were struck down with *pidinka*, a bacterial infection which caused suppurating wounds on the face. After these had healed, deep scars remained. *Rischta* was another common infection from the pool. It was caused by a microscopic parasite which bored into the skin to lay eggs – a form of scabies, extremely resistant to any cure.

Naturally, we did not dare drink of this water, and instead we had engaged a man to come daily with a skin of fresh water for our barrel. We were very content with this arrangement until one day I followed him to the well and found, to my regret, that it was located in the middle of the cemetery. After this discovery we began to boil our water. In any case, I preferred to still my thirst with fruit provided by the bountiful season in endless supply: grapes, peaches and melons.

On one celebrated occasion, Kalantarow the merchant invited us for supper. No doubt he wanted to show us a true oriental hospitality and to remind us that he was still the great merchant he had been in Samarkand – even though Bokhara required him to wear a rough woollen kaftan with a tassled rope around his girth. In Samarkand he had owned the city's most spectacular house, with arabesques of marble; the gardens, in season, had been a riot of heavily scented roses and other flowers. But his residence in Bokhara was no bigger than ours. We sat on the floor, on an exquisite Bokhara rug, waiting for his eighteen-year-old wife – our hostess. Finally she wafted into the room like a graceful swan, and we could only stare at this apparition. She was

134

classically beautiful. Her face was perfectly oval, and I felt myself drown in her great, dark, velvet-soft eyes. On her head she wore a diadem of uncut jewels, and the sapphires hung like droplets of blue water against her noble brow. Her ears were pierced with finely worked rings of gold, and these were laden with silver and gold charms, as well as pearls and coral. She was expecting her third child, and was heavily draped in salmon-pink silk. Over this she wore a light tunic of braided gold thread, encrusted with pearls. It was as if Scheherazade herself had stepped out of a fairytale.

Her mouth was as red as the coral in her ears, and its shape was infinitely delicate and fair, but not a word came from it. She knew only the Hebraic language. Or was she perhaps worried that a movement would spoil her classical beauty? Nor did she eat, nor even drink. In fact, during the whole meal she did nothing but exhibit herself to our engorged eyes – I have never seen a more impressive table decoration. Very occasionally, she tilted her head slightly, just to let us know that she was alive. Kalantarow was in his seventh heaven – he could see that we were dazzled.

A multitude of strongly spiced dishes arrived: fish stuffed with garlic, schaslik seasoned with berberis, minced doves with strange, unheard-of vegetables. Grapes, peaches, nectarines and apricots spilled over the sides of deep bowls of beaten silver. After the main courses came preserves of nuts, rose petals and violets, small hard ginger cakes that burned like fire in the mouth, and finally confectionary tinted with saffron and rose oil. The wines were rich and heavy as oil. Servants replenished our glasses constantly. Over this sumptuous excess, the languid and indulgent eyes of Scheherazade gazed out, focused on each and yet none of us, immobile and devoid of any conscious emotion.

135

'Feasts like this will be a thing of the past once Bokhara falls,' said my father to the host.

'Oh, the Bolsheviks will never come here,' the Jew objected. 'What would they do here?'

'Here is beauty, gold and jewels in plenty,' said my father with a little bow to the hostess. 'The Reds attach great value to such things. I know with absolute certainty that they are coming, and in the interests of friendship I am warning you of it . . .'

'These are just inflated rumours,' said Kalantarow. 'Stay here in peace and quiet. The whole of Turkestan has been encircled by the Reds. In this heat you'd be fools to travel. The way to the Aral Sea is not as forbidding as the desert, but you will not be able to endure the heat of the steppe. If you wait until the end of August, when the winds are cooler, you may also find that the cause of Bolshevism has cooled . . .'

'No,' answered my father. 'I must leave as soon as I can, and I advise you to do the same, my friend. I am grateful to you for your aid in finding camels and a driver, and for that reason I urge you, most sincerely, to flee!'

But Kalantarow did not want to hear any more doom-mongering. He clapped his hands and had his children brought in, so that we could admire them. Again he clapped his hands, and this time two young boys, fourteen or fifteen years old, came into the room. One of them was dressed in a heavy *khalat* of gold brocade. His face was painted and, like every other *batschi* dancing boy, his fingers were covered in jewelled rings. The other boy sat down on the floor and began to play a two-stringed instrument consisting of a long neck and a hollowed-out pumpkin. The *batschi* started performing an improper dance: his face remained absolutely still, while his body twisted obscenely. The presence of my parents heightened my embarrassment.

I looked at the ceiling, and my mother studied her nails. Only Kalantarow lauded the dance. He grunted and cried out with approval, all the while draining his wine glass and having it refilled. When he gave the sign for another dance, my mother stood up abruptly and we followed suit. By this slightly pre-emptive departure, we were spared any further displays of Bokhara ballet.

Much more to our taste was a dance we witnessed a few days later. Next door to our house there lived a Jew who was the father of three enchanting girls. The oldest was eleven, the youngest seven. They dressed in red ankle-length skirts. Their nails were also painted red, and their hair fashioned into a mass of thin plaits, the tip of each weighted with a silver coin. Sporo, Rahmail and Dorusch were their names. At first they were very frightened of us, yet they stood by our threshold like three wild, curious kittens. It was obviously irresistibly facinating to watch the outlandish manners of these foreigners. With time, they became increasingly bold, until finally they dared come into our house and speak to us. One day, Sporo came in with a tambourine. From her face, it was plain that she had something on her mind. Boris, who had the best hand with the children, asked if they wanted to dance for us.

No, quite the opposite! They wanted us to dance for them, while they played the tambourine. And preferably we should perform the same dance as yesterday. After much confusion, we grasped their meaning. Simply, they had seen us doing our daily programme of stretching and exercising, and they thought it a marvellous routine. We lined up, all six of us, and rarely can a group of keep-fit enthusiasts have had a more appreciative audience. They laughed and screamed with delight as we bent our knees and stretched our arms to the beat of the tambourine. Afterwards, we asked them to dance for us, and now they could not refuse us. Rahmail beat the tambourine and Dorusch clapped her hands, while Sporo did the dancing.

She moved her lithe little body with the most refined natural grace and sense of music. Her face was statuesque – as if formed in stone – but her figure gave the purest expression to the soul of the dance. Her little hips swayed, and her feet, which had never known the confinement of shoes, were like petals falling from flowers. The thin hands with lacquered nails fluttered around her body like so many butterflies, while her long black plaits tossed and the silver coins jangled to the rhythm of the tambourine and the handclapping of Dorusch. In this unconscious, childish dance, surrounded by attendant sisters, she was the very embodiment of the Eastern soul, a princess such as one can see in Persian miniatures. These little beings lived in their father's home as if it were a prison, and were already being readied for the life of the harem. When the tiny Sporo went to the bazaar, she had to wear a net of horsehair over her face. This she wore with the same pride that a European girl feels in her first grown-up dress.

At the end of July, destiny sent fresh trials to assail us. I sickened with malaria, as did Boris and Tamhina. Our little house suddenly became a hospital. Kalantarow often visited the convalescents, and he would sit cross-legged on my 'bed', trying to cheer me up. He promised that as soon as I was well, he would take me to the Sart fortune-tellers of the bazaar. I would be able to choose who among them should tell my destiny. The augurers of the Sarts were renowned for their skills at reading the book of the future.

I believe that this promise hastened my recovery, for within ten days I was walking with Kalantarow towards the bazaar. We looked at each of the fortune-tellers, and then I chose the most hideous one; I felt that a genuine sorcerer should look just like him, and this was probably correct.

He was crouching in a little niche below the Tower of Death, on a beautiful woven rug. Dirty folios were scattered all about him. His body resembled a skeleton, with skin stretched like vellum across his ribs. His face could have induced fear in a man of some courage. It had a strange hue, yellow and grey, with greenish shadows; from deep sockets, a pair of phosphorescent light green eyes stared out with piercing intensity. It was as if his whole being had shrivelled and died, but the eyes were still alive. There was not a single hair on his head, but a few desultory whiskers hung down from his chin. A set of long brown fangs protruded over his lower lip. Yes, this was the freak that I wanted!

We sat down before him, and Kalantarow gave him my name and birthday, as hoarsely requested. From the rags about his body he produced a dice. I shuddered when I saw his hands. He had exceptionally skinny long fingers, thickly covered in dark hair; I saw before me a pair of giant, hairy spiders every time he rattled the dice and cast it. Quietly he counted the eyes of the dice and referred to one of his folios. Then he began to intone with his dead voice. He did not stop talking for five minutes at least. Afterwards he fell quiet, and seemed to sink back into his lifeless torpor. Only the green eyes were still alive, still relucent with a fearful glow. Kalantarow put a silver coin on the mat, took my hand, and led me away.

'What did he say?'

'Well . . . he said that everything would go perfectly for you . . .'

'Was that all he said?'

'Of course.'

'But he was talking for a long time – five minutes at least!'

139

'Indeed he was. But to be frank with you, it was of no consequence at all. Everything he said was promising, and that's the main thing, isn't it?'

Suddenly, Kalantarow seemed to be in a hurry, and we walked back briskly. I lay for a long time, that night, unable to sleep. On the following day, the second caravan was departing. I could not rid myself of the infernal light I had seen in those green eyes. Even in my dreams they stared at me, and never once turned away. What had they seen? What had they read in the secret pages of time?

19

The Second Caravan

On the morning of 8 August, just after sunrise, all seven of us gathered by the south-western city gate. Our camels were ready to go. No outsiders had been told the hour of departure, to avoid the heart-rending farewells that had plagued our last exodus.

Boris and I were busy with our camel, still tethered on the ground. I had just related the episode of the fortune-teller, and Boris had responded that I should not worry myself with such nonsense.

He had hardly spoken his last word when the leading camel – with my parents precariously mounted on top – lunged on to its feet and snapped its tether. Bucking and lashing out with powerful hindquarters, its massive *hidjeva*s were jettisoned as if no more than a couple of matchboxes. My parents were thrown hard against the ground. They were dazed, but luckily there were no broken bones or signs of concussion. The problem was, simply, that the camels were too well rested. Camels can put up with anything apart from an excess of good living, which makes them obstreperous.

This incident was at once interpreted as a bad omen. A few of the Sarts shook their heads ominously, and Uljanow was whispering with the Czechs. My poor battered mother started crying, and at first my father did his best to comfort her. Then he cried out, 'What sort of foolishness is this! Aren't you ashamed of yourselves to be as superstitious as old peasant women! Get a move on . . . we have no time at all to lose!'

With this, our second caravan moved off. The camels, as we have already established, had been well fed and watered for some time; hence we moved with unusual speed. Nor was the procession very long: our driver, Jam-Baktschi, rode at the front on his donkey. Behind him, attached by the long rope, came my parents, followed by Boris and I; after us rode Bina and Tamhina, then Uljanow in his *hidjeva* balanced by a crate of foodstuffs. Last of all came the camel bearing the waterskins.

The sky was overcast and the heat none too pressing. Our spirits were high, and the misadventure by the gates already forgotten. We had a mere week of travel before us. This trip would be a bagatelle compared to the previous one. Besides, we were prepared for every eventuality. The water in my pot splashed to and fro; best of all, I had bought myself a length of rubber pipe, so I could take a pull of water whenever it was deemed necessary. I was proud of my invention. I also had a little volume of Lermontov's poems which I tried to savour between the jolts of our bumpy passage. This book had been presented to me as a gift by one of my Russian flames in Bokhara, whose heart I had captured with a few tunes on my violin.

Our first stop was in Hadji-Arif. It was a very lively little town, where an extensive horse market was in progress. Diverse races and tribes filled the streets. There were Sarts, Chiwini, Tajik people, Persians and Arabs. The Kirghiz were selling horses to finance their purchases of sugar, salt and flour – which would later be ferried back to their *yurts* on the wild steppe.

Within the hour, we were travelling over the Turk-istani steppe, flat as a pancake and wider than the eye could see. Not a tree, not a bush, or even a blade of green grass edified this harsh environment. Almost every day we passed by some Kirghiz *yurts*, invariably situated close to a well. These *yurts* were covered in felt as a protection against both the sun and the cold. The Kirghiz often invited us, with great show of hospitality, into their homes, where they offered us everything their poverty could muster. Fried camel meat was set before us – and, as expected, it proved rather tough! Camel milk was also served – it had a subtle salty taste, and a texture thick as cream. Sometimes they indulged us with their greatest delicacy, the Kirghiz *kumis*, which has been mentioned in an earlier context. This was a horse's milk which had been allowed to ferment in a leather sack.

It was impossible to get them to accept a single kopeck. In Bokhara I had bought a Russian-Kirghiz dictionary, and now I used it to make inept efforts at communicating. These gracious, hospitable people were highly appreciative, in spite of the veritable toads that must have issued from my mouth. My attempts never solicited anything but polite attention and surprise. At every *yurt* I enquired for news about the Bolsheviks, but people shook their heads and replied, '*Bolshevik jaman . . .*' Which, in translation, meant 'Bolshevik, bad man . . .'

The young women were often very beautiful, in spite of their wide, round faces, and their slit Mongolian eyes. Their sparkling gaze, dazzling white teeth, and peach-soft skin made them uniquely attractive. Constantly barefoot, dressed in nothing but ankle-length garments, their hair hung down in hundreds of plaits that tossed over their backs. The men, needless to say, treated them as dogs. Wives had to work like slaves. On one occasion, we witnessed a rich Kirghiz, the lord of three *yurts*, giving a severe beating to one of his wives. When Boris tried to dissuade him, the latter stared at

143

him with dumb incomprehension: could there be a valid reason for not hitting one's wife?

My mother provided endless diversions for the Kirghiz women. Often they enticed her into their *yurts*, where they tried to undress her, curious to know how she wore her garments. They pilfered as many of her buttons and pins as they dared. When they discovered her sewing box there were screams of joy. In a matter of minutes, the contents had been divided up. Three of the women got into dispute over ownership of a thimble. They smote and scratched each other like wildcats until the strongest emerged victorious. Triumphantly she pierced the trophy and tied it to the end of a pigtail.

As our caravan moved on, the women congregated outside the *yurts*; their dark eyes shone with goodwill, and their white teeth highlighted their smiles as their strange guttural cries sped us on our way. We felt very clearly that they were blessing us, imploring luck to be on our side.

Our progress over the steppe was swift, often ten hours at a time. The temperature daily touched 50 degrees Reamur, but we had finally become accustomed to it. Besides, we had our protective sun-screens. Every day we found a new well, and there was plenty of food. Why, this was almost a pleasure trip! No lice had come to suck our blood, and for this we were infinitely grateful. In a few days we would arrive. Life lay before us with so much promise that sometimes we raised our voices and sang a song to express our gratitude.

No more than a day's march remained when, one evening, we pulled into a medley of *yurts* that almost formed a village. A little spring teemed out of the ground and ran merrily between the huts. Its water was slightly saline. Our camels drank in long greedy draughts, and bellowed contentedly. Here we made our camp. All night, a pack of famished saluki greyhounds hovered around the edges of our fires. They snatched at whatever they could get, and fought over the bones after our evening meal. One of them dared come close enough to steal a big piece of goat's cheese just by my head. The moon, suspended above us, was blood-red. A dog howled while the rest of the pack whimpered in the darkness. It was a tragic, a foreboding sound. We were brusquely awoken during the early sunrise by a tall bearded Kirghiz standing in our midst, shouting in broken Russian. He told us to return to Bokhara at once. A matter of a few kilometres away there was a large body of men, Kirghiz Bolsheviks, more cruel than any other beings on earth. A week earlier, a few officers had tried to come through this way. They had been captured and tortured to death.

'Do not stay here any longer! Flee! Flee back to where you came from!'

The sun was not even high in the sky, but we set course for Bokhara without delay. No songs were sung; we sat deadly quiet on our camels. I felt as if a knife had cut my joyful heart from my breast; despair now had its throne there. Maybe Providence had already decided that we should never escape death. There could be no hiding place for us on the steppe, amongst the Kirghiz people; news of our whereabouts would always keep abreast of us. Instead we had to go back to a city whose fate was sealed.

No one urged the driver to make haste, and the return took ten instead of seven days. Why should we quicken our pace? Who, after all, would ever rush into the arms of Death?

20

The Trap

A bitter resignation and dumb despair characterised our return journey to Bokhara. Hardships were overcome, and feats of endurance performed without high-spiritedness. We were extinguished in our souls, if not our bodies.

Bokhara, however, was still free when on 25 August we moved back into the old house. We had hoped never to set eyes on it again; instead, we were once again sitting on the floor listening to the latest news from friends and acquaintances: the Reds were expected any day, and the Emir was ready to flee. Kalantarow was among the visitors.

'Remember the fortune-teller?' he asked me. 'I didn't want to sadden you by translating his predictions. He advised you against the journey to the north, saying that it would be no more successful than your previous attempt southwards. But . . . he said something else . . .'

'What . . . ?'

'He said that the "journey into the unknown" would bring greater rewards . . .'

I picked my wits, trying to understand what he could have meant by this. Had I not, on many occasions, heard old people talk of death in these terms? Thankfully, human beings have a talent for hopefulness that, within days of a major setback, rears its head like an insistent steel spring. We took new courage and set about looking for another route. Soon, the open maps were once again on the floor. We discussed alternatives, measured distances, and made plans. My father had sought the advice of camel drivers and prominent merchants whom he could count as friends. From these enquiries he had gleaned that there was one last untried route due west through the Kisil-Kum desert to the Caspian Sea. This very perilous expedition would take at least two months. And who could even guarantee that by the time we reached the Caspian shore, the Red Army would not already be there to greet us? Two months in the desert! From experience we knew the meaning of such an undertaking. To the north, east and south, hoards of Bolsheviks were closing in. Was there no road for us but the prescribed one to Khiva?

My father had an acquaintance whom he respected in the manner of a friend: Fazli-Alahi Fazliamedow, a wealthy tea merchant from Samarkand, and previously a business contact, was now also residing in Bokhara. He assured us that there was another possibility of escape, if we took our caravan south-east over Afghanistan – first to Kabul, then Peshawar, and finally to the Indian coast. In Peshawar, Fazli-Alahi had a brother; he promised to furnish us with a letter of recommendation to the latter, who would gladly assist us in all our needs. This struck us as a better plan, and my father determined to put it into effect. However, it could not even be contemplated without the permission of the Afghani authorities, and the appropriate documentation. To this end, my father went to the Afghan consul-general to present his case. Remarkably, the great man was at all times unavailable. Either he was engaged on official business, or he was away, or he had left instructions not to be disturbed. When my father eventually demanded an appointment, the consular staff suddenly lost their command of the

147

Russian language. After several failed attempts, a goodly bribe cleared all the hurdles in one fell swoop. The secretary, suitably enriched, became convinced that his master would see my father on the very next day.

The elusive consul was surprisingly affable, but he made it clear that all visa applications had to be submitted to the authority of the Bej in Mazar-I-Sherif. And he, in turn, would probably have to consult his own superiors. Indeed, the papers would have to make the rounds of several Afghani cities. Postal messages were conveyed by a horse-mounted courier who would need a week at least to reach Mazar. It quickly became evident that our passes could not be in our hands until October. My father made other visits to the consul, to see whether this procedure could not be hurried along, but he was told simply to relax, as there was no immediate hurry. The rumours of an impending attack from the Bolsheviks were all wildly inaccurate. He was advised to rest and prepare himself for the journey at hand. There was nothing for it but to arm ourselves with an oriental patience. Day after day passed, week after week. Patience was in short supply, but our anxiety was endless.

By a friend at the court of the Emir, my father was told in strictest confidence that the Reds had issued an ultimatum: all Russians in Bokhara were to be extradited at once. The Komissariat in Samarkand wanted especially to trace our family, as we were rumoured to have fled with millions of roubles in gold and jewels. The Emir had sent a reply that he had no knowledge of our whereabouts. As for the other Russians, he asked for a month to think it over.

A few days later, a certain Polish lady came to visit. She had learnt from an unimpeachable source that the Bolsheviks would attack Bokhara in fourteen days unless the Emir extradited all Russian refugees. The

Red Army lusted for plunder. The city was renowned for its rich Sarts and Jews, its gold and silk, exquisite rugs, and scores of harem women without compare. The first act of the occupiers, we were told, would be to train their artillery at the Tower of Death. The Emir's palace would be levelled to the ground. The building itself may have been of uncertain architectural value, but its contents must have been priceless. That the conquering of Bokhara would be a bloody affair was not in dispute.

And all this in fourteen days! It was time to act. We could no longer afford to wait for the Afghani visas. If our lives were to be saved, nothing remained to us but the western route to Khiva and the Caspian Sea. Uljanow explained that such a trip could only end in death. He intended to stay in Bokhara. He would rather be shot by Bolsheviks than slaughtered by wild Chiwini tribes. Poor Uljanow, he did indeed die as he had chosen, on the allotted day.

The rest of us embarked on immediate preparations for the third caravan. My father decided that camels had to be procured the very next day. He dictated a long list for me, detailing various supplies that I had to buy in the bazaar and apothecary. It was a very long list.

Early the next morning, the Afghan consul-general came to visit us in person. With a charming smile he informed us that, quite by chance, our passes were ready much earlier than expected. He handed over the documents and received the exorbitant, but statutory, fee. We could barely contain our relief. The only one to retain his calm, was my father. He put a hand against his heart, as is the custom in Turkistan, and bowed very low. The consul-general advised us to travel with camels until Mazar, and then continue on horseback over the mountains. Wherever we went, our passes would ensure the cooperation of local people.

149

At once, my father went to Fazli-Alahi to ask for the promised letter of recommendation for Peshawar. He related how the Afghan consul had honoured us with a personal visit, during which the invaluable passes had been presented to us. But Fazli-Alahi was troubled by the news. He thought the episode wholly out of character. The consul usually paid scant regard to the needs of other people. And besides, how could those passes have been produced with such speed? There had to be something sinister behind this! Fazli-Alahi had connections with access to the circles of the Afghan consul. These sources of information had to be tapped; he promised my father a true picture of events within twenty-four hours.

On his way home, my father walked through the bazaar; he met a few acquaintances, and they already knew that our passes had been issued, and that shortly we would be making our escape through Afghanistan. Once again, here was an example of how effortlessly news spreads in the East – as if by a covert wireless service. More surprises were in store for us. That same evening, the Afghan Consul presented himself at our door for the second time. It was plain that he could hardly contain his eagerness to have us gone – despatched on our way to Mazar-I-Sherif. He had come, he said, merely to advise us to leave at the first opportunity.

My father pretended to that eastern gratitude which knows no bounds; but as soon as our benefactor had gone, his expression became grave. Uljanow shook his head, but said nothing. Bina and Tamhina stared at my father, who was nervously smoking a cigarette. Suddenly he stood up and went out; in fact, he went straight to Fazli-Alahi, who was not at all surprised to see him so soon. He had already managed to find out what lay behind all these machinations of the Afghan consul-general. Afghanistan, it transpired, had in the last few days signed an anti-British alliance with the Soviets. To oblige its new ally, Afghanistan's government had indicated that all Russian refugees within its borders would be arrested and extradited back into the hands of the Bolsheviks. In other words, we were going to be the first instalment of this charming scheme. But if the Afghanis were clever, then my father was cleverer by half. Fazli-Alahi had a friend who took care of traffic between Bokhara and Peshawar. This merchant was commissioned with setting up a caravan to take us to Afghanistan at short notice. Thereafter, my father went to another driver, with whom he had already been in communication, and instructed him to equip a caravan for Khiva – but with the utmost regard for secrecy! Camels, stores and water were to be procured with all possible speed. A large sum of money impressed the driver with the benefits of keeping quiet, as further funds might then be forthcoming. Such pungent reasoning is readily understood by Easterners.

My father then announced to the Afghan consul that a caravan had been made ready for the passage to Afghanistan. The name of the driver was given. The consul immediately made sure of the information; by word of Fazli-Alahi, we found out that on the very same day he despatched a courier to the Reds to forewarn them of our arrival. If destiny had not played into our hands, we would have been riding into certain self-destruction. The whole of the Russian community believed that we were riding into Afghanistan, and we fanned the fires of these rumours as much as we could.

In the midst of these events, a group of prisoners of war arrived in Bokhara. They had escaped from Skobelew, and had resolutely marched for forty-five days across the steppe. The group consisted of Germans, Austrians, Hungarians and Czechs. All of them were in

151

a pitiful state: emaciated, sick and mortally tired. The Emir showed some compassion in offering them food, clothes and lodging, but he refused them permission to leave the city. He was concerned that the Soviets would accuse him of treason if he allowed prisoners of war to go free. However, as relations between the Soviets and Bokhara deteriorated day by day, the Emir soon realised that no possible advantage could be gained by holding these men back. Soon, he would make his own escape from the capital, this he knew all too well. His five hundred camels stood loaded, day and night, ready for the flight into Persia. And so he duly allowed the refugees to continue on their weary way. They, meanwhile, had found out about our caravan, which had become common knowledge in Bokhara. A delegation arrived at our house and entreated us to include them in our number and take them to Peshawar.

The more people we could bring with us on the actual caravan to Khiva, the better it would be. My father therefore promised that they could go with us, but he did not enlighten them as to the true route of our caravan. He let them believe that Peshawar was our goal and destination. But afterwards, he entrusted Bina and Tamhina with marching them across the desert to Kara-Kul, where our true caravan was being equipped for its assault on the wilderness.

All manner of obstacles impeded our progress, and the days slipped away. We were already in the month of October. The cold had come, and we had to purchase thick clothes and strengthened waterskins which would not burst if the water froze. Everyone who could was busy fleeing from Bokhara: Persians, Kirghiz, Afghans, or any other people who feared the outcome of the next few months.

At last word came from Kara-Kul. The preparations

were complete. Our followers were eagerly awaiting us, and the path to Khiva was beckoning. On 16 October we left Bokhara for the third time. Leading us was a friend of Fazli-Alahi, who had been initiated into our secret. His pack camels bore his wives, children and rugs. He too was departing Bokhara. Seeing us off at the gates were a few officials from the Afghan diplomatic staff; with false smiles they wished us a happy journey. No doubt they reported back to their master that his schemes were being put into effect, and that the Russian sheep were on their way to the slaughter.

After a few hours, we came to the place where, as arranged, a Sart on his donkey was waiting for us. He had been assigned to lead us to Kara-Kul, where he too would join the caravan. A hearty farewell was said to Fazli-Alahi's friend, who continued in a south-easterly direction towards Afghanistan. We kept waving until his entourage had disappeared over the horizon; and then we laughed at the thought of the long faces of the Bolsheviks, when this mock caravan arrived at the border without us – Afghanistan's first present to the Soviets. By that time, we would be well out of reach, deep in the desert of Kisil-Kum.

21

The Third Caravan Heads West

In Kara-Kul, no fewer than sixty-eight people were waiting for us, all willing to risk life and limb for a chance of achieving freedom. Those with money had hired or bought camels. The rest of them would travel on foot, including the forty prisoners of war.

There was an assortment of Germans travelling with us: the Schmidts (a pharmacist with his wife) and a couple called Stoltzer with two young children – one of three years and the other a mere six months old. They also had a lovely black dog called Bischan, who quickly made friends of us all. She was especially fond of a Hungarian prisoner of war called Biro; her loyal dark eyes did not leave him for an instant as she curled up next to him at the campfire. In addition, there was a group of Russians, amongst whom I saw a woman travelling alone.

The coward and bogus doctor, Kalantarow, had managed to inveigle himself into our midst, but happily his uncle Oboljanz was absent (apparently, he had opined that our expedition was suicidal). This was extremely fortuitous, as our driver was none other than his arch-antagonist, Hudaj-Verdy. Once more we had to entrust our lives to this wily old fox, but at least we knew that nothing could be expected from him. Our waterskins were as robust as they could be, on this third caravan, and our hearts had been equally hardened against undue optimism. Besides, there was no other driver to be had. Only Hudaj-Verdy had pronounced himself willing to lead us. He gave us an evangelical smile, mesmerised us with that heavenly gaze, and swore his dedication to our cause. Extending his hand to my father, he gave credence to this pledge with a regal composure. However, we pointedly did not ask how long it would take to get to Khiva. We knew from bitter experience that the Sarts had no concept of time and space.

On 17 October, then, we headed off for the Amudarja River, which had to be forded. Heat no longer plagued us; quite the contrary, the days were cold. At night, the temperature plummeted to freezing point, and we slept in little coteries, huddled together to stay warm. The sand was hard and cold, touched by white frost as we woke up at sunrise. The air was clear as crystal. Even at noon the temperature seldom rose higher than 10 degrees Reamur. At first we were gladdened, our minds still preoccupied with recollections of thirst and heat. Soon, such thoughts were banished as the mercury sank further and further in the thermometer.

In spite of the weather, we were almost as thirsty as during the hot season. Water, therefore, had to be rationed. I scoured our plates with sand. It was forbidden to use water in matters of personal hygiene. No one even shaved, so that, after a few weeks, the caravan consisted largely of bearded ragamuffins. We had a plentiful supply of pomegranates, which were as if created for the desert. The husk is as tough and dry as leather, so that the rich juices retain their flavour and freshness. A pomegranate has the unique ability of singlehandedly quenching a serious thirst.

The road we took was well-known to us. Soon we greeted the sixteen trees which stood as green and inviting as the last time we beheld them. It was like

155

seeing a gathering of beloved friends. On the following day we reached the banks of the Amudarja, at a point midway between Ildjik and Ak-Robat. The gleeful name of the latter town was misleading, for Ak-Robat was full of Bolshevik spies, as was indeed Ildjik. However, there was no immediate cause for concern as we were only staying long enough to satisfy our thirst. Loading would begin almost immediately. In spite of misgivings, the yellow water was delicious, as on the previous occasion.

We spent almost an hour in fraught negotiation with the Chiwini, who were demanding fantastical sums of money to ferry us across. They felt unable to perform the task for less than 1,000 roubles per person. At this levy, the whole caravan would cost at least 72,000 roubles! One of our negotiators began to harangue them in round Turki syllables, but he fell quiet when the Chiwini resolutely approached him with drawn knives and murderous eyes. Someone else tried to explain that we were not Bolsheviks, but poor Germans. Germans were considered to be very poor. In the end, after lengthy debate, we agreed a price of 7,500 roubles for the whole caravan.

Towards evening, winds blew up; frothing waves ran high on the river. The same wide-bellied flat barges were in use, but this time it took the whole night to get everyone to the opposite bank. The boats dipped violently in the rough breakers, and most of us became nauseous. As for the camels, they made an intolerable row; whenever the spray of the waves lashed against their bodies, they bellowed with anguish into the obscurity of the night. On reaching the shore, they were allowed to drink as much as they wanted. A camel can take in enough liquid to sustain it for five or six days at a stretch. As the caravan moved on, I could hear the water splashing in the belly of my camel.

156

And, in truth, the same sound issued from my own innards!

The original intention had been to hug the river and continue towards the north-west, but Hudaj-Verdy dared not pursue this course. The Bolsheviks seemed to have spies everywhere. He preferred to make a southerly diversion, and to travel in the comparative safety of the deep desert. The cold intensified until, suddenly and with deep regret, we had to admit that it was winter. The waterskins froze solid and had to be thawed out by the fire when we wanted to drink. As ever, we had to sit doubled up in the *hidjeva*s, with insensible, dormant limbs. At times we had to grit our teeth not to cry with pain. A dull pain was present in arms and legs, and rheumatism was no merciful travel companion.

Things got worse. A tenacious storm buffeted us for several days, occasionally working itself into a hurricane, and then declining into a strong constant wind which lashed icy granules into our faces. Once before, the wind had treated us to red-hot needles. Now it was selecting the ice-cold variety. We could no longer say which was the worst. Our throats and ears were encrusted with sand. We had to endure the whole downward spiral of suffering that a desert storm inevitably forces on the traveller. I tied a handkerchief over my face. The sand penetrated our clothes, tormented our skins, found its way into the mechanisms of watches, rendering them useless. Furthermore, the flour sacks were riddled with it, so that the bread at mealtime was crunchy and almost inedible. At its worst, the storm seemed to make the whole desert boil. The sand was in perpetual motion. In minutes, the terrain was transformed. Ridges and hills were blown away, and dumped elsewhere. The desert was like a tumultuous sea.

Then, at the very height of the storm, Hudaj-Verdy compounded our difficulties by losing the trail. The caravan zigzagged and circled, with no reference points to fix our course. Only the stars could enable our driver to find his way, but for five nights the skies were hidden by an opaque cloud cover. Five long days we wandered in the desert. Finally, Hudaj-Verdy decided that the search was whimsical and futile. The camels were drawn up in a great circle and, having tethered them, we made camp within the protective ring of their bodies. The evening ration of porridge tasted as foul as stewed sand, if this can be imagined. After this delicacy we crawled into our blankets like mussels into their shells.

When morning discovered us, the worst of the storm had passed. I lay buried under such a thick drift of sand that I had to be dug out. Towards evening, the skies cleared, the stars showed themselves, and we found our way back to the river, where the empty waterskins were replenished. A few kilometres back from the banks, we made a brief halt to rest. There were a few *yurts* nearby, from where we noted a distinct hostility. We saw some tall men; their shaggy fur hats made their stature seem even more impressive. Their eyes shone with animosity in weatherbeaten faces. They fingered the hilts of long daggers in their girdles. No one invited us inside, no one offered to share their victuals with us. Quite the contrary, in these parts all supplies had to be purchased at swindling prices, and any service had to be dearly bought. These Chiwini, however, who glared at us from afar, did not even approach our camp. Instead, we received another more notable guest: Death.

Biro died in the evening. He had been ill ever since we left Bokhara, where he had gorged himself on fruit, starved as he was after his long march. Kalatarow had diagnosed his illness as dysentery. The pharmacist, Schmidt, found no suitable drugs in the communal first-aid box, over which he presided. The last few days had been especially taxing for Biro. All we could do was to lower him down on to the ground; he was grateful to be spirited away by death, even though he would never again see his homeland.

We dug a grave and put his body into it. The wind soughed melancholically as one of his countrymen read a prayer. The grave was refilled to whimpering cries from Bischan; eventually she lay down on the little mound. When the caravan moved off, she followed us for a short distance, but was ever called back to Biro's resting place. Eagerly she yelped and barked to remind us that we had left him behind. Bischan was probably Biro's last and best friend on this earth.

Suddenly, the little Kalantarow came running up to my father. He was pale as a sheet, and even his knees were trembling as he told us what had happened: he had been called over to the Chiwini and taken to their leader. His name was Sultan-Murat, and he was a renowned bandit and close associate of the Khan of Khiva.

Through Kalantarow, this bandit chief was now sending his ultimatum to us. He demanded a thousand roubles, a watch and a pair of galoshes. If we did not satisfy this demand, he would ride ahead of us, collect his men who were all in the vicinity, and return to slit our throats. It was not an ambiguous message, and we decided to comply with it in full. One of the prisoners of war had managed to extract all the sand from his wristwatch, so that it was nominally functioning. He donated it for the common good, as a third of the ransom. Another man was in possession of a pair of almost brand new, shining galoshes. My father contributed the thousand roubles. Kalantarow took the booty to Sultan-Murat. One receiving it, the latter mounted his horse and galloped away. None of us even saw him go, but it was reported to us.

159

If we had already met with robbers and, to make things worse, robbers who were on excellent terms with the Khan of Khiva, how then would we fare as we probed the interior and approached the Khan's capital? It seemed improbable that our lives could always be so easily saved by the timely gift of a pair of galoshes.

The sensible option, to avoid getting lost a second time, was to stay close to the river. However, given that other perils were more immediate there, we took the precaution of tying rags around the camel-bells. The ensuing silence was highly irregular and perplexing to our ears, accustomed as they were to a constant ringing from dawn to dusk. We advanced through a thick belt of sedge and reeds so tall that our camels were completely hidden. Hudaj-Verdy was exhausted, and seemed to be actually asleep. His donkey was also, very sensibly, taking the opportunity of having a snooze. Its steps were slow and hesitant. The reeds became more and more impenetrable, and at last the whole caravan ground to a halt. It cost us a lot of pains to get out of this jungle, for camels cannot be induced to move backwards. One by one, they had to be led out. We found our way to firm sand, which now in morning was dusted with a layer of white frost. Our clothes were damp after a long misty night, and the sun was too weak ever to dry us out.

As we rode, I scoured the heavens for my favourite star. When it rose, I knew that morning was imminent; then, and only then, could we descend from the *hidjeva*s, collect firewood, kindle fires, and thaw out our aching limbs. And only then would there be cups of steaming hot tea. But just as the delicious warmth began to fill the body with well-being, the lice would make their inevitable assault. A love of warmth, alas, is an integral part of the louse's being. The whole caravan, animals and humans, was infested.

160

Fortunately, tiredness defeats even physical discomfort, and at long last we sank into oblivion. Our sleep was merciful, our tormentors forgotten. The mild morning star hung in the sky, keeping watch over the wretched men and women below.

22

Sultan–Murat

Suddenly, in the vastness, there was a procession of thin dark lines against the clean horizon. As we drew closer, we saw that they were telegraph poles. All about them hung the ragged remains of the wires. To us it was a beautiful sight: the first sign of a European civilisation we had not known for weeks. Nearby was a little town with the grandest caravanserai we had hitherto seen. It was teeming with people and their beasts: camels, horses, donkeys. As always, there was an open courtyard at the centre, and here a great log was smouldering and giving out a pleasant heat. We set about making tea. Kalantarow busied himself with the fire. Then, transfixed, his eyes met with a sight that overwhelmed him. Something in his hand fell clattering to the ground. At last the power of his voice returned, and he managed to say, 'Look over there . . .' He indicated, with a trembling finger, a man seated like ourselves with a bowl of tea in his hand.

Under a low brow, and almost hidden under the trimming of his imposing fur hat, a pair of flaming black eyes rested unembarrassed upon us. The nose was bulbous. A pair of blood-red lips shone from beneath his thick beard. He had calm but authoritative eyes, accustomed to being obeyed. We instinctively felt his power. Who could he be?

'Sultan-Murat!' Kalantarow, still terrified, enlightened us in a whisper. Finally, then, we were seeing our bandit. A sequel to our previous meeting seemed inevitable. We eyed him curiously. He stood up, lashed a horsewhip against his boot, and approached us.

'Good day,' he said benevolently, 'and welcome . . .' My parents responded courteously, but I burst out in surprise, 'Do you speak Russian?' He nodded, not without a trace of self-satisfaction. In his wild and uncouth appearance there was something childlike, primitive and faithful, which made us sympathetic towards him in spite of his earlier deed.

It must have been a mild and merciful power that gave my father the inspiration to greet our enemy with greatheartedness. This insight, as we later understood, decided the whole outcome of our endeavours and our flight.

'Sit down,' my father said, 'and be our guest . . .' Sultan-Murat stared as if his ears had deceived him, but he did eventually sit down, very slowly. When my mother handed him a bowl of tea with solicitous care, he took it bashfully and looked down at the ground.

'*Spasiba* . . . thank you,' he mumbled, and drained the bowl in a single gulp, although the tea was scorching hot. Then he looked up, and impulsively grasped my father's hand firmly as he broke into a repenting monologue.

'Sultan-Murat is sad. Sultan-Murat is bad man! Sultan-Murat does not want to be bad man . . .'

It was my father's turn to be surprised, but our guest did not give him time to respond. He continued in the same entreating vein, in his halting Russian, his eyes brimming with remorse.

'Sultan-Murat took thousand roubles, took watch and galoshes. Sultan-Murat the devil himself!'

163

'Not at all,' my father cried, to calm him. 'Sultan-Murat received these things as gifts . . .'

On hearing this, the bandit literally exploded with delight. He slapped his knees, thumped the clay floor, and such shrieks of joy issued from him that the whole yard reverberated. Kalantarow, who had slunk away at the approach of the robber chief, peeked out timidly from behind a camel.

'You are a fine man to say so,' our ecstatic guest continued. 'Sultan-Murat has sharp eyes, keen ears. Sultan-Murat notices that you are a fine man, your *mamashka* fine woman, your son fine son. Sultan-Murat was not fine man to demand thousand roubles, watch, galoshes. But thousand roubles I've eaten up, galoshes were too small, and the watch is broken for I poked to find the devil in it. Sultan-Murat not only a bad man. Sultan-Murat stupid too . . .'

So sincere and full of self-loathing was he, that my father immediately stretched out his hand: 'Not at all . . . forget that it ever happened. From here on we shall be good friends . . .'

Sultan-Murat took the proffered hand, and thereafter shook hands with me and my mother. He behaved with the solemnity of a man taking a holy vow. The handshake was symbolic: from this moment he would be our friend for ever.

'Sultan-Murat is your friend. Sultan-Murat shall protect you . . .' he said. And, in truth, time would teach us the significance of a promise made by an Asiatic robber chief. In the evening he returned carrying an outdated rifle and asking what we thought of it. Boris, an expert on firearms, examined it and told him that there were certainly newer models to be had; furthermore, it needed cleaning. My father brought out his little Browning and showed it to Sultan-Murat, who took it with fond eyes. The small, nickel-plated object was

164

turned reverentially in his trembling hands. He licked his lips, and was almost panting as his fingertips stroked the butt of the pistol with an uncertain tenderness. Then, in spite of the bitter regret in his eyes, our new friend returned the pistol to its rightful owner.

'Do me the honour of keeping it,' said my father.

There was boisterous protesting at this. 'But Sultan-Murat bad human! Sultan-Murat does not deserve such a rich gift!'

'Nonsense,' came the answer. 'Now please take this gift as a token of our friendship . . .'

Sultan-Murat snatched back the pistol and ran out of the caravanserai as if he had gone mad. Then we heard the crack of a few shots. He came back with the Browning in his hand. His face was a veritable lamp of joy; and his manic smile revealed strong white teeth. He nodded at my father. 'It's decided. Now Sultan-Murat wants to be general of your caravan. Great caravan without general is bad caravan. Sultan-Murat is a general, and so all will go well. Have you enough food? If not, Sultan-Murat will get as much as you require . . .'

We replied that our supplies were ample for all our needs.

'Now my friends must sleep as peaceful as in their own house. Sultan-Murat shall watch them . . .'

Not for a long time had I seen my father as happy as he was that evening. We all felt that we had gained a powerful protector in one who previously had been our enemy. And from this day Sultan-Murat did take on the task of commanding the caravan. It was curious to see how this unbending man, self-willed and hard as iron, knew how to gain power and respect from seventy-two exhausted desert travellers. Soon we had entrusted him with our lives, without a moment's doubt in his abilities.

165

We moved much more quickly than before. Sultan-Murat rode his horse up and down the caravan, along the ranks of plodding camels, and shouted out his orders. If necessary, he gave the Sart drivers a taste of the whip. This was an infallible line of reasoning which swiftly made them admit that Sultan-Murat was a mighty lord indeed. Even the audacious Hudaj-Verdy put his hands against his stomach as a sign of humble submission. He dared neither stop nor start the caravan without orders from the general. Soon nothing at all could happen unless Sultan-Murat had commanded it.

This wild bandit was a born leader with a magical ability to bend people to his will. But at the same time he was a great child. Sometimes he rode at the head of the caravan and, hollering like a naughty boy, fired his new revolver at the sky. Then he tucked it back inside his shirt; at nights, he slept with it next to his skin. Already on the first evening he rode with us, we had an indication of his priceless experience: he forbade us to make camp and light fires, informing us that on the other side of the river lay the town of Petroalexandrowsk, held by Bolsheviks. Our fires would probably have attracted a patrol to investigate, and this would have been the end of our journey. Furthermore, he made detours around most towns, and he knew exactly where it would be safe to stop. For rumours of our caravan always preceded our coming – passing from town to town, and across to the 'Red' side of the river, via Chiwini merchants.

From time to time, fearsome riders passed us by; they threw greedy eyes at our caravan, but when Sultan-Murat hailed them, there were cries of recognition and welcome. He invariably told them to deliver the following message to the Khan of Khiva: that we were approaching, and should be expected. Everyone in the desert seemed to be his friend, but if we met with people he did not trust, then they were subjected to a different treatment. Vengeance and death and eternal bad luck were promised by Sultan-Murat if they dared breathe a single word to the Reds of our whereabouts. People became half-crazed with fear; they knew that Sultan-Murat always kept his word. He, meanwhile, never honoured anyone but my family with his company, and never addressed other members of the caravan. He was full of deep disdain for all of our followers. But his horse was often found jogging along next to my parents' camel, and at these times Sultan-Murat would converse with my father.

'Sultan-Murat not a good man,' he said on one such occasion, 'but he is not always stupid. He has seen Taschkent, Samarkand, Bokhara and Kisilsu, and he has seen many people in his life. You say that the people of your caravan are German . . . but a few are Russian . . . and the little doctor,' he growled, pointing at Kalantarow, 'is Armenian, a filthy Armenian. Because you have taken him into your caravan, I shall never slaughter him . . .' Sultan-Murat spat contemptuously towards Kalantarow, who ducked into his *hidjeva* and made himself invisible.

On another occasion, he told us about the fate of eight Austrian refugees who had arrived in Khiva, six months earlier, on their way to the Caspian Sea. The Khan had received the Austrians well, given them clothes and food. Two of them had decided to show their appreciation by repairing the electrical pylons, which – as he put it – owing to the inadequate attentions of a miserable Armenian, were in a terrible state. When the Khan got such clear proof of their uncanny abilities, he refused them permission to leave Khiva. They should stay behind and keep an eye on his massive dynamo!

The remaining six Austrians managed to find a driver and continue their journey towards the Caspian Sea. *En route*, the driver's rifle jammed badly, but the Austrians serviced its faulty mechanism, whereupon the driver – giving them no hint of his intentions – led them back to Khiva. There, without delay, they were installed as superintendents of the Khan's armoury. Presumably, Sultan-Murat told us this story to forewarn us of the dangers of displaying any overt talents to the Khan. Within days now, we would be in Khiva. Sultan-Murat insisted that we would be expected, in accordance with the messages he had sent.

'What is this pot you carry?' he asked suddenly, pointing at a clay vessel in my father's *hidjeva*.

'It is sheep fat,' my father replied. 'We fry our pilau in it . . .'

Sultan-Murat gave him a crafty look and laughed heartily. The day after, one of the drivers walked past, and pointed at the same pot. 'Money money,' he said with a grin.

We became alarmed; the pot did indeed contain a quantity of my mother's pearls, and jewellery worth a small fortune. Over these valuables we had poured molten fat – and this, evidently, had now become common knowledge. At the next *yurt* I bought a thick loop of camel wool, which the women are forever busily spinning. This I wound around the valuables. It became a big tight ball of wool, which I kept between my legs in the hidjeva. Sometimes I pretended to be knitting some socks, to justify the presence of the wool; and at night I used it as a pillow. Sultan-Murat, having become our friend, was undoubtedly the only one in the caravan we could trust.

His name was like a magical spell in the land we travelled through. Whenever we halted near some *yurts* or a little village, the inhabitants stood outside their meagre dwellings and bowed so low that their heads almost touched the ground. That is, as soon as they

168

discovered the identity of the caravan's leader. Sheep and chickens were slaughtered. We were invited to come and sit by their fires, to warm our frozen limbs inside the *yurts*. No courtesy seemed too great for our protector. Sultan-Murat was now so attached to us, he explained, that he would not be parted from us in Khiva. He was planning to accompany us all the way to the Caspian Sea, and if the long arm of Bolshevism had already invaded those parts, he would lead us into Persia. Nothing was too difficult, no undertaking was too great.

'And I, Sultan-Murat, shall see to your needs in Khiva! You shall have money, warm clothes, and food from the Khan. Trust in me . . .'

He had an especially soft spot for me. When he had eaten his pilau, and there were some scraps left, he often called for me: 'Little son . . . little son . . . come and eat pilau with Sultan-Murat . . .' Usually, at times like these, he rummaged in his saddle-bags and produced a handful of raisins, or an apple, or some pieces of sugar. One night, I remember, we were in deep conversation. I was lying between him and my father in a *yurt*. A whole night's sleep lay before me. I luxuriated in the warmth, trying to forget the tiny creatures moving under my shirt and testing the thickness of my skin.

'When we come to Khiva, you shall stay behind,' Sultan-Murat told me. 'But your parents shall move on . . . they must! Sultan-Murat will tell the Khan that you are a good boy. Exactly what the Khan's small son needs to learn the Russian letters . . . no one in Khiva can write the Russian letters. You shall have own house . . . own rifle . . . own wife . . . or two or three if you like it . . .'

He said this so seriously that I truly believed he was in earnest, especially when I recalled the fate of the Austrians. Perturbed, I sat bolt upright and stared at

169

him. He glowed with pleasure at my reaction, but I saw at once by his eyes that he was playing. Sultan-Murat could never dissemble, he always gave himself away. To keep him amused I pretended to believe his every word, and he grew ever more animated. He bit his lip to stop himself from laughing, when I asked how big my house would be, and how my wives would look.

'The fairest among women you shall have. Their eyes shall be round and blue-black like plums with much juice. And their waists shall be of small girth, as thin as their heads! With breasts as big as this!' He gestured wildly. 'Yet firm! And wide hips that sway when they walk. Like this!' And he jumped to his feet and pranced about in the *yurt*, swaying his hips to show me the delights that awaited the future Russian secretary. 'And small children you shall have. Many! And all of them shall be boys!'

I could no longer keep my sober face straight. I exploded, and my laughter was like a dam being opened. Sultan-Murat's laughter broke over us like a mighty river. He laughed so that our ears were deafened; he screeched and hopped with glee like some giant in a fairytale. It took some time for us to enter into sleep's kingdom, for all our tiredness had been laughed quite away, and Sultan-Murat was a brilliant teller of his adventures.

By now, the fourth week had gone, yet several days still remained before Khiva – in the estimation of our general. Anyhow, we seldom even asked where we were, for our spirits were disabled and lazy after such long and torturous monotony. The nearer we came to Khiva, the more barbarous the natives seemed: their hats were even taller than before, their knives wider in the blade, and their eyes spoke of nothing less than a thirst for blood. However, we learnt that under this craggy, harsh exterior, there was a nobility far more worthy than anything we had discovered in the hearts of Bokhara men or Sarts. If we hailed these natives with smiles as they passed us by, they reciprocated by laying a hand on their hearts and bowing. But the sternness of their faces did not change.

Another source of wonder for me was in the unimaginable variety of camels: brown, black, pale yellow, dazzling white! Camels with one, two, or three humps! Some so long-haired that the fur obscured their legs and touched the ground. Others almost bald, or neatly clipped. And I saw magnificent riding camels trained to move without a rope piercing the nose. It was a fine sight to see such animals come at a gallop through the desert, faster than any horse.

Yet the desert itself was changeless as ever, nothing but sand to be seen, crowned by a great sky. It was always a relief to encounter a *yurt*. In some of these dwellings there were countless children, who lived as little swine and never washed – like their parents, they had no notion that water could be used for washing. The majority of them were infected with syphilis, their eyes sticky with pus. We drank from their cups, ate off their plates, slept on their felt mats. It was a miracle that we all remained in good health.

At some of these villages, Kalantarow announced to the locals that he was a doctor, and arranged open-air surgeries. In long queues they stood, these unfortunate people, waiting for their turn with the 'doctor'. They were charged for the initial consultation, and then sold medicine consisting of saline water or acetylene powder. Kalantarow took payment in silver and gold. As soon as my father realised that the Armenian was a charlatan, he threatened to report him to Sultan-Murat. Naturally, Kalantarow viewed this as unwarranted interference in his legitimate doctor's practice, but merely the name of Sultan-Murat was enough to close 'the surgery' for

171

good. By this stage, our resilience had become almost mythical. One day an icy rain fell until we were soaked; compounding it, a punishing wind rose out of the north. By evening, our clothes had frozen to ice, so that we crackled like dry leaves every time our bodies jolted against the sides of the *hidjeva*s. The prisoners of war were almost beaten; they hung like limpets alongside the camels, and occasionally fell down and had to be helped to their feet.

We stopped as soon as we found a hamlet, and spent the night in some *yurts*. The stink inside was unholy; the dirt lay in piles. Never before on this journey had we seen such human swine-huts. But the advantage of the *yurts* was their warmth, and we ignored our reservations and threw ourselves around the fires. The next day was the thirtieth of our journey; I was sitting in my *hidjeva*, as ever, rattling forwards at the same old pace, when I discovered a host of purple stains on my hands. I rolled up my sleeves and counted up to twenty similar blemishes. My father, when I called to him, told me to look at my chest – and the same symptoms prevailed there!

Within minutes, the whole caravan had discovered that it was similarly afflicted. Kalantarow, ever the doomster, began to howl that we had caught typhoid or the plague. His fears proved ill-founded; it was discovered that some fleas of unusual toxic properties had marked us with their bite. An unbearable itching started to plague us, even though we were accustomed to much suffering of this nature. Thereafter, the bites swelled into suppurating boils. We grew feverish. It became a day of pure discomfort; the hours passed in oblivious fever.

Sultan-Murat was of course free of infection, as were all the Sarts. No creeping thing could in any way embarrass them. Our general did what he could to raise our dampened spirits, but we were too depressed even to notice his efforts. But at dusk he suddenly cried out, joyfully. We raised our heads and saw, at the horizon, a strong and unusual glow. It could not be the rising moon, nor a star. An intense, cool sheen met our eyes. Before we could even ask, Sultan-Murat reined in his horse. He threw out his hand and said, proudly, 'Khiva!'

23

A Thousand and One Nights

The great ramparts of the city gates reared up against the
dark sky. The rust-red bricks were fiercely illuminated
by electric lamps perched high up, and beneath, the
whole city had come to witness our arrival. The eight
Austrians were especially eager to see us, and their joy
was immeasurable when they verified the presence of
countrymen in our caravan.

Great shouts of joy reached our ears from afar, and as
we drew nearer a whole detachment of retainers sprang
forward, as if on cue, to help us dismount from the
*hidjeva*s. Next, we were ushered through the arched gate
and into the city streets towards an imposing building
whose windows were streaming with extravagant light.
We were shown into a central banqueting hall, also
brightly lit, through lesser chambers though still of
estimable size.

The floor was covered in priceless carpets. The largest
was a hundred square metres, and the very colour
of blood. I have never seen its like in Europe. All
seventy-two of us were easily accommodated in the
great hall. The carpets were decked with brilliant faience
dishes – there were mounds of the finest pilau, rice and
roast mutton, heavenly white bread, fruit, and sweets
in plentiful supply.

Sultan-Murat was our host; he was certainly in his
element as he welcomed us in the name of the Khan,

whose honoured guests we were. With a magnaminous gesture he invited us to help ourselves and not be bashful about it. On this point we were only too willing to make a literal interpretation. Sultan-Murat moved freely among us and egged us on, urging us to eat more, and clapping his hands to hurry the servants bringing green tea and sweets to round off the feast.

The great room bathed in lavish light, the glowing deep-hued rugs, the retainers in picturesque uniforms, the surfeit of exquisite food on the bright platters, the hum and cries of joy from the assembled travellers of the caravan, lousy and pitiful; and in our midst, the romantic and glamorous presence of Sultan-Murat, radiant with benevolence like some desert prince! Was this not another story of Schehezarade, re-enacted in this place? I took such greedy pleasure in these sights that at last I began to doubt the veracity of my own eyes. Spurred on by intense emotions, my fever rose and made the blood churn in my head. Quinine made an infinitely better medicine than these stirring sights, and a large dose of it soon had me sleeping. Many of my comrades had already swooned away on the soft carpets, surrounded by dishes and debris.

The following morning the fever and harrowing itch had gone, and the boils began to burst. As soon as we were fit for it, we made an excursion to the bath-house that Sultan-Murat had earlier recommended. It was an oriental bath of time-honoured design, with a changing room afforded light by a few niches cut into the roof. Through these gaps came some rather sociable doves, who perched next to us and left their calling cards on our clothes. Next door was the principal washing room; its cisterns held hot water in plentiful supply. The abrasions left by parasites stung terribly, but it was nevertheless a true pleasure to pour basinfuls of water over our heads and to soap our bodies; afterwards we

175

felt like new beings, and we looked at the city with fresh eyes. No one was able to enlighten us about the origin of the enormous house where all seventy-two of us were billeted. Most rooms contained no furniture and no pictures, but innumerable carpets from Khiva and Bokhara adorned the floors with vibrant colour. Never before or since have I seen such a collection of carpets.

Sultan-Murat visited us a few days later, and with a secretive look he invited us to take tea with him. He noted with satisfaction our stunned surprise when we were led into some chambers with golden rococo furnishings and upholstery of dark blue silk. This had to be the best room in the house! It had been prepared for the last Russian Czar on the first and last occasion of a state visit to Khiva. In this showpiece apartment there was also a blue-painted pine dresser, such a one as could be found in any Russian kitchen, costing no more than five roubles. And on the gilded table was a ceremonious display of fur caps, each of them on an individual stand. The fur had been combed into neat curls.

We were amazed by this European opulence with Asiatic additions; and Sultan-Murat was visibly pleased with the effect. He served us tea while seated on an ornate gold chair. It made a curious impression on us, seeing this Asiatic robber chief in the milieu of Louis XVI. But within a few moments, the over-elaborate style of the surroundings became too much for our friend. He slid down on to the floor and crossed his legs; soon, our conversation was flowing more freely. My father wondered how long it would be before we could continue on our journey. Sultan-Murat exhorted us to rest and be at ease.

'Eat and sleep, sleep and eat! Much meat, much fruit, much bread, much tea. Ask Sultan-Murat for anything, he takes care of everything. Nothing shall cost any money. My friends are the guest of the Khan . . .'

176

The road before us was very long, and our caravan had to be equipped for winter. So, not wanting to be boorish, we took our friend's advice. Each day we were served ample meals by a group of servants. Mutton, vegetables, rice and delicate waifer-thin bread were set before us at lunch. And in the evenings we supped on raisins, milk, tea and small aromatic melons – within their green skins the flesh was snowy white and replete with syrup-thick juice. The prisoners of war were in paradise. Many years had passed since they last had access to such plenitude. Their incarceration in Russia had been terrible indeed.

On the other hand, none of us had ever been subject to such infinite and tender care, nor had even dreamt that such liberality could exist. And this from a people renowned for their cruelty and bloodthirstyness. There were others who praised the generosity of the Khan, although, in a sense, they lived as prisoners in his city. These were the Austrians. When they had left the Khan for the first time, he had donated camels, foodstuffs, furs and money. Had they not foolishly mended that rifle in the desert, they would have been back by now in their own country. Instead, they were living in Khiva as the most uniquely honoured men. The Khan provided them with everything they wanted, even women – but he denied them freedom. In response to his largesse, they had repaired and serviced the Khan's armoury and his one artillery piece. And, to top it all, they had supplied the whole of the city with electricity. With commendable foresight, they had trained a few Armenians to mind the enormous dynamo, and now lived in hope of accompanying us.

We longed to be able to thank the Khan personally for everything he had done. One day, Sultan-Murat indicated to my father that the Khan wished to grant us an audience. He received all his suppliants in a modest little house, where he sat in a fair-sized room sumptuously transformed by another brilliant carpet. An old man of sixty or so, he was of small stature, with a weatherbeaten face and a grey beard; but he shone with benevolence as he extended his hand to my father, who had fallen on his knees, as etiquette demanded. Behind the Khan stood an adjutant, with a rifle between his feet. Sultan-Murat, even he on his knees, did his duty as interpreter. Later, he told us that the following words had been exchanged.

First of all, he had his own say: 'This is a very good German . . . in Samarkand he was a man of wealth and power. He was a great man, and yet he had to flee the Bolsheviks with his family. The prisoners of war go under his protection. I have led them here so that you can help them continue . . .' At this point, the adjutant added his sentiments to the conversation. 'Certainly you must help these people . . . imagine the sufferings they have endured to escape our enemies!' Sultan-Murat continued, 'They are impoverished and tired. The majority do not own a single tenga. But you are rich and mighty. You shall help them. You shall give me money, and I shall furnish them with furs so they do not freeze to death in the wilderness. Their food supplies are small, and their camels are bony and weak. They were provided by Hudaj-Verdy, who has tricked them many times before, and who has taken money in payment from them. This dog should be soundly whipped. And if you do not help these good people, you draw a great and notable shame over your name. But substantial sums of money will be required to pay for camels, provisions, furs and fur hats. And the prisoners of war have gone on foot the whole way, so that their boots are in shreds. To them you must give new boots, and camels . . .'

The adjutant, who evidently was a friend of our interpreter, echoed his sentiments persuasively. 'Yes, Sultan-Murat speaks the truth. God shall surely reward you in heaven, and forgive your sins, if you do this . . .'

This last argument seemed to have clinched the matter. The Khan clapped his hands, despatched a servant on an errand, and entertained himself with Sultan-Murat until another retainer came with a roll of banknotes and several pouches of coins. He waited for his master to give him the go-ahead, and then he gave the money to my father. An amicable nod from the Khan concluded the audience. Any thanks or words of gratitude, he did not want to hear. The banknotes were in 500- and 1,000-rouble denominations. They were of Chiwini variety, printed on silk, which was harder wearing than paper. In all, we had been donated no less than 17,000 roubles.

My father called a meeting of all the travellers in the caravan, and told them about his visit to the Khan. No one would believe him until he actually showed them the royal gift. Then, in the midst of the jubilation, he handed the money to Sultan-Murat and entrusted him with administering the needs of the caravan. More importantly, he asked him to remain as our general. Sultan-Murat was deeply flattered by this, and wasted no time in taking my father to a lesser, tributary nobleman.

This man was treated to a long speech about our requirements, and every sentence was peppered with discreet threats and indications as to the repercussions of not helping our cause. This provoked an immediate response of generosity. By these unorthodox means, a further 6,000 roubles were added, in the form of a reluctant gift, to our swelling coffers. My father, as before, entrusted the money to Sultan-Murat – whose shrewdness was only redeemed by his good heart!

Hence we all began to view Khiva as an enchanted city. Only Hudaj-Verdy, who considered that his efforts had gone unrewarded, was not content. However, when he got news that Sultan-Murat had urged the Khan to have him whipped for past treacheries, he did the wise thing, and evaporated with his Sart henchmen.

Thanks to the invaluable help of our general, our winter caravan was soon fully equipped. Fresh camels stood waiting in a nearby village, Il-la-ly; the road was not long, and so we went on foot while luggage, provisions and furs were loaded on to a big *arba*. On this occasion I saw another side of Sultan-Murat; I had almost forgotten that he was a Chiwini robber, cruel and bloodthirsty, and not only the jovial friend for whom every day I thanked God and our lucky stars. When the attendants had finished loading the *arba*, the driver mounted the horse and took the reins. Sultan-Murat told him to get down and walk, as otherwise the load would be too heavy. But the driver took no notice of him.

'Can't you hear what I'm saying! Get down, dog!' Still the driver did not move. Sultan-Murat, agile as a cat, climbed on to the shafts and flung the unfortunate man into the ground. Descending with a whip in his hand, Sultan-Murat ordered the servants to strip the man of his shirt and kaftan; then he let him taste the whip, which was tipped with a piece of metal. Strips of flesh were torn from the naked back. The servant lay immobile and made no sound as the blood poured off him. It was a hideous sight. About thirty Chiwini calmly witnessed the flagellation. When Sultan-Murat thought his victim had had enough, he put down his whip and walked away through ranks of men that respectfully stepped aside for him.

Il-la-ly consisted of a medley of smallish huts, a bazaar, and several large caravanserai. We congregated in a yard where a man had hung a saucepan of boiling oil

180

over the fire; in this, he deep-fried fish brought from the Amudarja. It was crisp and delicious, and a mere tenga coin secured a large portion. A long time had passed since we had tasted fresh fish.

We stayed in Il-la-ly for ten days, while Sultan-Murat procured some especially robust waterskins. One day we were honoured by a distinguished visitor. He was eleven years old, rather thin with pale yellow skin, and dressed in a kaftan, lacquered boots, and a tall fur hat which rivalled him in stature. He appeared suddenly in our caravanserai, accompanied by a group of twenty boys of his own age. He was, in fact – since the death of his older brother – the Khan's oldest son, and hence the heir to the throne. Without much ado he sat down on the ground and explained to Sultan-Murat that he had come to have a look at me. Fascinated, he stared and poked at me in an explorative manner. I thought him an unsympathetic prince. Having asked my name, he demanded, 'How many wives does Jascha have?'

I laughed at this, and explained that amongst my people, boys of twelve do not take wives. This surprised him excessively. Every five minutes, some boy from his retinue set a big waterpipe before him – and, with much coughing, he sucked at it. After him, the other boys took turns to smoke the same *kaljan*. They mimicked every movement of their young ruler, and repeated, like a chorus, every word he spoke. Once answers had been obtained to his curious questions, he wanted to show me his might. Ostentatiously, he took hold of the youngest boy present, held his hands fast, and slapped him across the face until the poor blighter was crying. The latter, however, made no attempt at self-defence, and when the prince's arm grew tired, he released the boy and grinned at me triumphantly. Then he ran like a whirlwind out through the gates of the caravanserai, followed closely by the screaming swarm of twenty boys. It

181

occurred to me that he was a thoroughly unorthodox crown prince!

That same evening while we were sitting in our new fur coats by the fire, Sultan-Murat came running to tell us that the Khan had news from Bokhara: the Bolsheviks had stormed the city, razed the Tower of Death, plundered the bazaar and executed all the Russians. The Emir was in flight to Afghanistan with his harem. There was complete silence around the fire. Then, for the first time, I saw my father cross himself.

24

Goal in Sight

There was no time left to lose. Already on 26 November – the day after the previously described events – our caravan was ready to set off. It was reassuring to see the line of forty camels, all of them exceptionally doughty and strong, their swelling humps bursting with amassed energy. Proudly, and yet with a certain indifference, the camels gazed out across the desert – man's greatest enemy – as if they had nothing to fear from it.

We climbed into the *hidjeva*s and waited for the general's orders. No one was travelling on foot. Sultan-Murat rode his impeccably groomed black stallion up and down the ranks, inspecting his work with satisfaction. The camels and donkeys were first class, the ten accompanying servants were trustworthy. Most importantly, we had boundless confidence in our general. He gave a cry, and with a jolt the little bells started ringing. Within a few hours, we had left Il-la-ly's huts far behind us and were deep in the desert of Kara-Kul. Sultan-Murat could not tell us which way he would choose. Chance would have to determine our road. The power of the Red Army was spreading in all directions; a town that was White today might be Red tomorrow. But our general reassured my father, patted his back, and promised that within two weeks we would reach some White stationhead on

183

the railway line to Krasnowodsk. The Caspian Sea was still in Imperial Russian hands, of that he was certain.

The real winter had set in. It snowed constantly, and our waterskins were turned into unwieldy lumps of ice. But, thanks to our thick sheepskin coats, fur hats and untanned boots, we were spared additional hardships. Winter gave us cause to remember the Khan's gesture with gratitude. We journeyed all day until six in the evening, when we stopped and made a fire for the night. There was a troubling shortage of fuel. We made use of dried camel dung scattered around old, abandoned camps. Food could be cooked on such a hearth, but its glow was too meagre to warm us.

The apothecary's wife worked the hardest at gathering fuel. All of her life, her husband confided, she had lain on a sofa, nursing her poor nerves; in the cold clear air of the desert, he had watched his wife turning into an energetic and resourceful woman. Our nomadic existence had acted upon her like a stay in a sanatorium. That first evening she stood and watched as my mother gutted a great fish. A smaller fish was discovered in its belly, and at the sight of it, the sentimental apothecary's wife burst out tearfully, '*Armes fischlein! Es was ein Weibchen!*'

Episodes like these were highly appreciated; laughter was the only elixir available to us, as most of our thoughts still hovered around the possibility of failure. After our meal, we settled around the fire, only to be disturbed by the customary scourge of caravans – lice. The camels being unusually well fed and powerful, they had brought a plentiful supply of the little pests. Soon, as ever before, we had clawed ourselves bloody on legs and chests. Under these conditions, sleep became a restless affair. At midnight, Sultan-Murat woke us.

I can still hear his strong, authoritative voice, calling through the darkness. 'Up! Up! People get up! Onwards! Ooooonwards . . . !'

We sprang up, rolled up our blankets, and began to load the camels. The moon shone brightly on the sand with its glistening coat of frost; it was bitterly cold, so that the ropes used to lash down the loads often snapped like brittle whisps of straw. The camels got up, protesting and trampling, the prisoners of war quarrelled and accused one another of pilfering matches or water; one could not find his saucepan, another energetically cursed the lice; sometimes there were brief fights between the men, and sometimes weeping and homesickness. There was an abominable row until we finally got away. It must be said that the prisoners of war complained far more than the women of the caravan. I never heard my mother moaning, unless it were with pain; and Frau Stoltzer, with her two small children to protect, was just as brave – it was not easy for her, shivering in a narrow *hidjeva*.

At daybreak we stopped to bake bread and boil rice and tea. Before too long, food supplies had diminished until we had to make do with one meal per day, the customary bowl of rice and fat. Permanently hungry, our bodies lost any surplus weight. Conversations were exclusively devoted to gastronomy or Bolsheviks – the greatest good and the lowest evil. After fifteen hours of rattling in my *hidjeva*, I might suddenly hear a voice in my ear, speaking with utter clarity. 'Cold ham with mustard!' or, 'Roast duck with apples . . .' I assume that this must have been some kind of hallucination, for Boris could not have been so cruel.

One day our general gave the ominous order that all pots and pans should be filled with as much water as possible. We were heading into terrain where not a single well or spring would be found for six days.

185

Soon after, we arrived at the dried-up riverbed of the Usboj, where previously the Amudarja had flowed. At some point in the past, it had burst its banks and changed course so that now it emerged in the Aral, not the Caspian Sea. Its former course had become a deep ravine with such sheer slopes that we had to dismount and walk, while our camels slid down on their haunches. The bottom of the ravine was covered in fossilised crustaceans. After laboriously climbing the opposite bank, we discovered a dramatically changed landscape. The sand was gone, and in its stead the ground was level and hard as if made of packed and dried clay. It would have made an ideal track for cyclists, who could have effortlessly pedalled over this plain for mile upon mile.

One of the Hungarians, perched on the very top of a load borne by a pack animal, was unfortunate enough to fall asleep and, in the ensuing fall, dash his head against the ground; he concussed himself so badly that, within a few hours, he was dead.

As it was impossible to dig a grave in this place, we wrapped his corpse in a blanket and left it, temporarily, in a *hidjeva*. That same morning he had been sitting with me at the campfire, telling me of his wife's mouth-watering capsicum goulash, and the joy there would be in his home in Budapest when he reappeared alive and well. His wife and five children would hardly be able to believe it. Within a few days he was sleeping in a shallow grave beneath a sandy dune. His manner of dying, a few paltry days before reaching his destination, was meaningless and unfathomable.

Then, one night, having pitched camp by a little hamlet with a few *yurts*, and fallen asleep by the fire, we woke by habit at midnight – but there was no Sultan-Murat urging us to rise. Deliciously, we sank back into slumber. The next morning we rose and boiled

186

some tea. Still there was no sign of Sultan-Murat. What could this mean? My father went in search of him, and found him in a *yurt*, seated on the floor and surrounded by prattling Chiwini.

'It's time to set off,' said my father, but Sultan-Murat's face grew dark. 'What's happened? Is something wrong?'

After a morose silence, Sultan-Murat finally explained that we were within a few kilometres of the White station Djabel on the line to Krasnowodsk.

'Dear God, how wonderful!' my father burst out. 'Let's make all speed to get there . . .'

'Not yet! Sultan-Murat has to think . . .'

'Think! What is there to think about? Who knows when the Bolsheviks will take this station too! Let's hurry up so that we can get a train to Krasnowodsk!'

But Sultan-Murat shook his head in displeasure, and continued to discuss matters with his countrymen, taking no further notice of my father who was staring at him as if struck dumb.

Suddenly, Sultan-Murat turned towards my father and cried furiously. 'Russians bad! Bolsheviks are bad, but White Russians are bad also!'

'What do you mean?'

'Chiwini tell me White Russians take their camels and money. Take our camels that I shall return to Khan. Take also the horse of Sultan-Murat. White Russian, because of war with Bolshevik, take the horse and eat the camels. Therefore Sultan-Murat is in no hurry to go to the White Russian . . .' When my father returned and informed the caravan that we were within a few kilometres of Djabel, there was mad celebration. The earth itself seemed to be burning under our feet. We rushed up to my father and asked him to explain the delay.

At this moment, Sultan-Murat emerged from his *yurt*. His face was morose. 'Camels are tired, camels need

rest,' he pronounced. 'Camels wait here a few days . . .'
His words produced an immediate reaction: there was a
good deal of crying and shouting. Some were furious,
others despairing.

'Wait a few days! A few kilometres from our goal?'

'Don't we have a will of our own?'

'Let's go at once! We have to go at once!'

Then, as if on cue, a distant explosion of artillery
silenced us – fearfully, we listened as its rolling echo
spent itself in the expanse of the desert. But Sultan-
Murat, without losing his composure for a single
moment, nodded ominously at us and said, 'Bolshevik
is fighting White Russian sixty verst beyond Djabel.'

'Why not then make haste to reach Djabel before the
Bolsheviks occupy it?' my father cried.

'No,' came the insistent answer. 'We wait here a few
days. Camels are too tired if something happens . . .'

He had barely concluded his words when the can-
nonade resumed and continued for several hours, inter-
spersed with the crackle of bursting grenades. Boris, as
an experienced officer, could estimate both the calibre of
the artillery pieces and, more importantly, their range.
He considered them to be closer than sixty verst.

It was unbearable to wait, and to have to listen
to the hellish concert, especially as the explosions
were beyond the horizon, leaving neither tracers nor
smoke. In the end we were nervously pacing about
the camp, counting each explosion as it came. The
apothecary's wife punctuated each salvo with a nervous
little shriek. But the camel drivers sat by their fire
drinking tea in peace and quiet. These momentous
affairs had little to do with them; they let the camels
stray at will in search of thistles. Sultan-Murat remained
in the *yurt*, conferring with the Chiwini. We knew his
mood well enough not to interfere with him. A few
of the Austrians who could not endure the nervous

188

tension set off on foot to reconnoitre the terrain around Djabel.

Already by morning they were back in camp, and reported that White soldiers at the stationhead were expecting the vanguard of the Red Army at any moment. Every moment was precious. With a burning sense of purpose, my father went to Sultan-Murat again. For several hours he begged and cursed and implored him in every way to take us to Djabel. If he feared for his camels, could he not then take us within walking distance, and let us make the last kilometres on foot? But Sultan-Murat insisted that by now it would be better to wait. If necessary, he could take us to Persia.

Faced with this possibility, my father redoubled his efforts, and then, at last, our truculent general gave way, came out of his *yurt*, and ordered the drivers to prepare to move. This was easier said than done. The camels had been loose for two days, allowed to eat and drink at their leasure, and now they wanted nothing to do with ropes and reins. They screamed, kicked and snapped at their masters when they felt the loads on their backs. It took until evening to prepare for departure.

Sultan-Murat came to my father and asked him to write a short message to the Khan of Khiva. He wanted this as proof that he had led the guests of the Khan to their goal.

'You shall write on the paper that Sultan-Murat has done his duty, and for this you are grateful to the Khan . . .'

As my mother had the best handwriting, she crouched down on a mat in a nearby *yurt*, and proceded to write according to my father's dictation. When the Chiwini saw a woman who could write, they called for their wives. These emerged from their *yurts* wearing nothing but flimsy white gowns, and came running barefoot over the freezing ground. Shivering with cold, they

189

howled with laughter when they saw this 'learned' woman daubing strange symbols on the paper.

Sultan-Murat took the letter and tucked it into his inside pocket. Then he clasped my father's hand and said, 'Sultan-Murat's soul is very heavy. Sultan-Murat has a bad soul. Sultan-Murat has taken a thousand roubles, a clock and galoshes from friends. In God's name, you must not remember it . . .' With great emotion, he swung into the saddle and gave the starting signal.

My parents had barely eased themselves into the *hidjevas*, when their camel tore itself free and bolted off with a mighty roar. It galloped faster than any horse, but my parents held on tenaciously, believing that their last hour had come. Two brilliant riders managed to capture the enraged beast after a wild pursuit across the steppe. The camel kicked and fought, and tried to break its bonds again. By the time my mother had dismounted, she was close to fainting. She announced, quite categorically, that she had no intention of ever again riding on a camel. She kept her word. For the rest of the journey she walked, and my father walked by her side.

All night we heard the barrage in the distance. The explosions sounded nearer and nearer. We should already have made Djabel, but the camels were making very slow progress, probably on the specific orders of our general. My father asked for an explanation, but Sultan-Murat would give him no answer. From the opposite direction, a great caravan, *en route* for Khiva, met with us. It belonged to a fabulously rich nobleman by name of Anna-Khan, who rode at the head on a large camel. He exchanged a few words with Sultan-Murat and immediately ordered his caravan to halt. Thereafter he introduced himself to my parents, and presented them with a sheep which was duly slaughtered and roasted.

190

Anna-Khan sat down with us around a fire; when he noticed my mother sitting on the bare ground, he called for a servant, who came running with a little carpet. This, he insisted, she must keep as a gift; we were highly impressed by his generous nobility.

Anna-Khan spoke impeccable Russian, and he gave us up-to-date news from the frontier. The Red Army was indeed closing on Djabel, but it would probably take another three days before they had it in their hands. On this score we could be completely at our ease, for we would be there within a matter of hours. However, the small town of Kisil-Arvat had been taken, and the artillery we had heard related to the storming of a smaller station further up the line. Should anything go wrong, he assured us, Sultan-Murat would willingly lead us into Persia – this, as an option, was highly unattractive to us. Our wanderings in the desert already seemed interminable to us. When Anna-Khan departed from us, he gave my father a highly unusual gift: two packets of cigarettes. This was unexpected, and very welcome. He wished us the best of luck and then, with servants and staff all about him, continued on his way. Seldom if ever had we seen such a gracious man, nor one who travelled in such style.

Thus, on 15 December, our caravan set off on the very last stage of its journey. I thought that the camels were dawdling, but it may have been my excitement playing tricks with me. The artillery opened up again, but soon fell quiet. The stillness of early dusk settled over the plain. A slushy rain began to fall, but I hardly noticed it. I was oblivious to the cold and the fatigue, the lice, and all the fiascos of the past months. My poor mother struggled along bravely at a respectful distance from the camels, who kicked anyone who ventured too close. Even Bischan, the dog who had shared all our hardships, barked and hopped with

191

renewed energy, as if conscious that our ordeal was almost over.

It was dark already. The evening breeze had died down, and the snow was falling in big white flakes. I shut my eyes and tried to envisage a locomotive and a train, a station. I imagined I could hear the sound of a whistle.

Then hoarsely, Boris said: 'Can you hear something?'

'No. Can you? Cannons?'

'No . . . listen carefully!'

I listened until I thought my ears would burst, but all I could hear were the ever-present camel bells: their constant tinkling choir.

Once again, Boris asked: 'Are you deaf? Can't you hear it?'

I strained, and finally did hear something which brought a cry of joy to my lips. I cried like a mad-man, emptying my lungs. And then our whole party registered what we were already aware of – the puffing of a train up ahead and, as a climax, the sound of a piercing whistle from the locomotive. No music, no song, no tender words could produce quite such a heavenly effect as this harsh scream that shattered the desert's blanketing silence. An electric charge passed through the caravan. The camels quickened their gait. Hypnotised, we stared into the wall of darkness until we saw the lights of Djabel. There was great jubilation. They shone palely, and yet to us they were brighter than any star and seemed to flood the whole desert with radiant hope. At six o'clock the caravan halted. We were then close enough to see people moving on the lit-up platform.

Sultan-Murat was reluctant to go any closer. All our luggage was loaded on to three camels. The remaining animals were taken back to the camp where we had stopped with Anna-Khan. Sultan-Murat even took the precaution of sending back his horse. The ten drivers made their farewells, and entreated us to forgive them if they had not 'been as we should . . .' In this moment, any possible grievances were forgotten; my father gave them generous gifts, and we left them with a sense of emptiness. Sultan-Murat's misgivings proved to be well-founded. On arrival at the station he was immediately arrested by the commanding officer; however, when my father explained that we owed our lives to him, he was released on the spot. Sultan-Murat came into the waiting room where we were temporarily camped. He fixed his eyes on me, and said with great sadness. 'Are you glad now, little son? Now you can go to your Germans . . .'

A gentleman entered the hall and presented himself to my father as General ———. I was surprised that he wanted to make himself known to us, for after all these nomadic months we looked far from pleasant. No one had shaved since Bokhara, and hence all the men had wild, bushy beards. Our faces were caked with dirt, and we looked like rough natives in our fur hats and coats. But evidently the general was a man of some courage. He invited the four of us to his home, which consisted of a railway truck, where he had lived with his wife for the past three months. They had made use of this truck to escape from a nearby town, through a veritable rain of bullets, the evidence of which was clearly visible all over the walls. We were given tea and rusks, and kept each other royally entertained with stories of mutual suffering. It must be admitted, however, that we were a little concerned lest our charming hosts should discover the lice coming to life in the pleasant heat and crawling over our fur coats.

These worries were soon forgotten at the din of an approaching aeroplane and the explosions of flying bombs. The general's wife was not noticeably affected.

It was a shame, she remarked, that one's sleep had to be disturbed by 'such a racket just outside one's window . . .' The general could give us no information about the next departure for Krasnodowsk. He was awaiting orders on the wireless. The train would leave at first opportunity. He advised us to pack ourselves and our luggage into a few cargo trucks waiting on the line.

We did so. In all, there were thirty-five of us, with a great number of trunks. We stood or sat like herring packed into a barrel. It was not even possible to scratch oneself, which in the heat became a matter of urgent necessity. I simply could not hold out any longer, and so I slipped out and lay down on the cutting, close to the wheels, so that I could quickly hop inside if we moved. Unfortunately, many of the prisoners of war followed my example. As they lay down next to me, I registered an upturn in the parasitic activity. Finally I gave up, joined a Turki at a nearby fire, and managed to beg a cigarette from him. He rolled one for me, then another, and then another; all the while, he kept me entertained with horror stories of the Reds and their various atrocities. This kept me awake until dawn, when people in the goods wagons woke up and climbed out. They could hardly believe that we were still in Djabel – they had set their hopes on waking up in Krasnowodsk.

That morning, Sultan–Murat came to take his farewell of us. He was as unsentimental as possible, which made the procedure short and less painful than it might have been. Yet, his eyes were full of undiluted sorrow. In a low voice, he bid us forgive his past deeds; then he pressed our hands tightly once more, before turning back to the desert and heading off with long strides. Not once did he turn around to wave, but we stood

194

and watched him until he was a tiny dot on the horizon which then faded away.

As a robber and an enemy he came to us, but as a helper and friend he left. I shall always use your name with gratitude, Sultan-Murat.

25

On Course for Freedom

In the evening we packed ourselves into the goods wagons a second time; sleep must have overtaken me, for I woke to the rhythmic sound of wheels rattling against the track. Soon the welcome sound had roused our whole company and there was light-hearted banter all around.

Four hours later, the train pulled into Krasnowodsk, and we had our first glimpse of the dark green Caspian Sea. The town was in the process of a gradual evacuation in the face of the Red Army's advance from the east. Some abandoned barracks were made available to us, as a temporary home. We hurried out to buy food, but most of the shops were closed, and we could rustle up no more than bread and dried fruit. What we did find, however, was a bathhouse with plenty of hot water. We went there with great relish. Having cast off our sullied desert clothes and dived into the pool, all three of us – Boris, my father and I – shot up bellowing with pain. The hot water came from some distilling works where, in the absence of any local wells, the salty waves of the Caspian Sea were transformed into drinking water. The surplus hot water was pumped into the pool, along with a great quantity of amassed salt. Our skin being practically in shreds after the month-long attention of parasites, the saline water burned like fire. My mother, who was in the women's pool, fainted with pain, and

196

had to be carried out. Standing there like white pillars of salt, we hoped that the lice would not develop a taste for salted flesh, having already proved their liking for the raw variety.

A cargo ship took us aboard for the passage to Petrovsk; however, two dear friends had to be left behind. One of them was Boris, who had immediately been mobilised when he presented himself to the authorities. He stood on the quay, pale and thin as a rake in his uniform, waving goodbye. Next to him was the faithful Bischan, howling with despair at this unlooked-for separation. The captain had steadfastly refused to have an animal on board the ship – and Boris had had to promise to fend for her. I am certain that a portion of our tears were for her. Shared danger, sorrow and adversity tie the knot of friendship with a more abiding strength than can be found in happiness.

It was very heavy to see the last of Boris. My own sufferings, and the events of the following years pale into insignificance when held up against his terrible experiences at the front, in Gallipoli! More than once, Death stood by his side, but his hour of destiny had not yet come. In the end, all human sacrifice became meaningless, and he fled to Europe. There, in the city of Prague, he finally achieved his ambition of graduating from the university with a doctorate in astronomy. These days, Boris resides in Algiers, and from the observatory of the French State he studies the vibrant African skies. This is a good place to take our leave of him.

On 22 December we stepped ashore at Petrovsk and proceeded at once to the railway station to enquire about connections across the Caucasus to the Black Sea. Some of the worst panic I had ever seen held sway in this station hall; there was constant running and vociferous skirmishing between incensed passengers. Every ten minutes or so, a major scuffle broke out between a couple of hot-headed antagonists; their antics were completely disregarded by other travellers. The only real issue was to get hold of a ticket and fight one's way on to a train.

On the floor of the second-class waiting hall lay a dead woman with open, punctured eyes and a gaping mouth; death, however, was too common to be respected, and travellers stepped over her as if she were a sack of straw. Our train was leaving on the following morning, but it was always inadvisable to trust such information. Hence we sat down next to hundreds of others, and waited. SLEEPING IS FORBIDDEN IN THIS STATION a placard announced hopefully, but it hailed from a different era, and was no longer relevant.

Before the sun had even risen, my father went to buy the tickets; there was already a long queue stretching from the ticket office right back through the station hall. My mother and I dragged our belongings, stashed in a few sacks, on to the platform, and waited by the train. It was rapidly filling. Our fears grew by the minute, for there was no sign of my father. Then, no more than thirty seconds before the train was set in motion, just as the whistle sounded, we saw him come tearing down the platform with three tickets in his hand. He had managed to clear a passage towards a carriage when the stern conductor appeared in the doorway and gave him a shove in the chest, crying: 'We're full . . .!'

'Ten thousand roubles for a compartment!' my father cried.

At that very moment, the train started. The conductor took hold of my mother and hauled her inside. My father threw me after her, and then managed to get himself and the sacks aboard just as the train gathered speed. The conductor got his ten-thousand-rouble note.

We were given his own booth, which was intended for one person only. Nearly all our friends from the caravan were on the train, but none took any notice of us. It was enough work taking care of oneself, without making a fuss about anyone else. Hence, there was no opportunity even for farewells.

For hour upon hour, the train coursed through the Caucasus. As we passed into tunnels the sudden air pressure dislodged unfortunate passengers from the roof. Penniless stowaways had no choice but to travel thus. I had heard such screams on another occasion; no one paid any attention to them. In Ekaterina the conductor opened the door of his 'cabin' and had to help us out – for we had been so uncomfortable that, uniquely, our limbs had slept while we kept vigil. Here, we had to change trains. Once again, there were wild races down the platforms, bouts of fighting and shoving; the conductor in the new train was selling seats in the lavatories for thousands of roubles. A mere 3,000 bought us seats in a second-class compartment. This accomplished, I was despatched to buy some food; I managed bread, ham, butter, apples and a bottle of wine – all at grossly inflated prices. My father, pleased with this haul, lifted me in through the window of our compartment.

And the train rolled on through the Caucasus; the wheels made their steadfast rhythm. 'Can you hear what the train's singing?' my father asked. 'Saved – saved – saved – that's what it's singing. Now that we're out of the Bolsheviks' hands we may as well get out of Old Russia too . . .' He laughed for the first time in many days, and my mother reciprocated with a smile. Then, we consumed the delicacies I had bought. My father uncorked the bottle. We made a toast and wished each other a merry Christmas, for it was 24 December. The Caucasus treated us to an

199

unceasing dance of beautiful Christmas trees outside our window; as dusk fell, a burning bright star appeared in the sky, and there were joyful hails and cries in all the compartments. It was indeed a vagrant Christmas for refugees.

At one o'clock in the morning we arrived in Novorossijsk, on the edge of the Black Sea. The festive atmosphere evaporated at once, for the platform restaurant had been converted into a hospital, and through the plate-glass windows one could clearly see the sick and the wounded lying in rows, on the floor and in beds. Soldiers from the front lay there, some newly operated upon and in considerable pain. Others were dying before our very eyes; we had been informed that both cholera and typhoid were rampant in the Caucasus, and had ample proof in the afflicted victims we saw amongst the soldiery.

It was a terrible Christmas night, but we had nowhere else to go. A venerable old woman on the train had warned us not to venture into the city by night; people were constantly being robbed and gunned down in the streets. Temperatures plummeted as low as minus 15 degrees Reamur, and we sat along the walls of the hospital, constantly aware of the harrowing misery within.

At first light, my father took a horse-cab into town. We remained sitting in the cold, anxious for him. But he was back within a few hours, bursting with good news: he had been at the Danish consulate, where the consul-general turned out to be an old schoolfriend. Using his influence, the latter had managed to book us three first-class tickets on an Italian steamer, the *Leopolis*, which was departing for Brindisi in two days. We trooped off to the consulate to thank the consul personally for his help, but as we came through the door, the staff retreated apprehensively.

We must have loooked terrible indeed in our dishevelled furs. Dirty, long-haired, thin, and my father with an unkempt and filthy beard. As soon as their fears had been put to rest, we were shown a disarming and touching courtesy. The consul-general took us into his apartment, and we had invigorating baths in his marble tub. Then we doused ourselves in naftalin so that finally we could be rid of the lice. Another cab took us into town, where our hair, and my father's unflattering beard, were given over to the fastidious care of a barber. We even purchased new clothes, disregarding the fantastical prices – for the value of the rouble had fallen significantly. Even the cabdriver saw fit to charge us a thousand roubles for a half-hour ride. These new clothes made us feel like mannequins, and we stared at one another, overawed by this sudden elegance. My formerly corpulent mother looked like a slender young lady – she had lost sixteen kilos in the desert. There can be few women who would have been able to endure such a radical diet!

To celebrate this civilised day, we went to the best restaurant in town and ordered just the kind of meal that had figured in our obsessions around the campfires. This was ill-advised. Our stomachs, accustomed over a period of months to rice and sheep fat, could not digest the rich fare of a normal European cuisine. We were punished with painful hiccups that lingered for several days.

On 30 December we boarded the *Leopolis*. Our modest cabins seemed to us the very height of luxury. There were clean white sheets, polished mirrors, and basins with running clear water. It was strange and wonderful to lie in a bed after so many nights in the sand.

By New Year's Eve, the *Leopolis* is already far out at sea. We are sitting in the galley, plotting on a map the exact distance of our journey from Samarkand. It corresponds to a line from the southernmost tip of Spain to the northern extremities of Europe.

One morning we are standing on the deck, looking out across the prow. In the far distance, at the narrow mouth of the Bosphorus, we can see the shimmering towers of Konstantinopel. Tightly, we press each other's hands. Words are superfluous. My mother sobs at the happiness which floods her heart so amply. Now, Konstantinopel is etched clearly against the brightening sky. And here my 'golden road' from Samarkand must come to an end. For mile upon mile it passed through sandy deserts, hence its famous name. But to me it was precious and golden because the loyal pursuit of it brought life's most necessary commodity into my hands. And that thing, of course, is freedom.

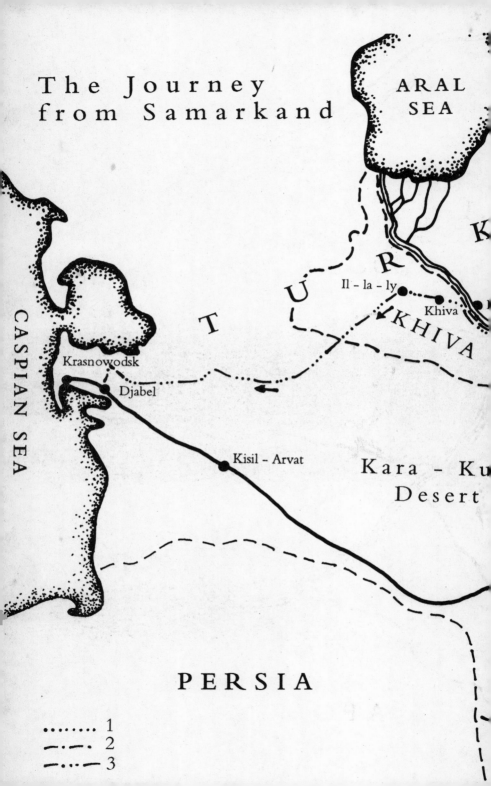

The Journey from Samarkand

ARAL SEA

CASPIAN SEA

T U R K

Il – la – ly

Khiva

KHIVA

Krasnowodsk

Djabel

Kisil – Arvat

Kara – Ku
Desert

PERSIA

········· 1
─ ·─ · 2
─ ·─ · 3